**"Stay here** [...]
**could be n** [...]

She nodded and watched as he disappeared. Without his weight keeping her arms down, Cassie was able to reach up and touch the scar on her neck.

Then she dropped her hand to her stomach.

Henry's voice joined the chorus of the law enforcement in the diner. It had been so long since she'd heard it like this. Panic and determination. Fear and anger. Uncertainty and planning. And then there Henry was, among them, adding to the group. It had been over seven months since she'd seen him. Now there he was after no contact whatsoever.

And still he'd tried to protect her.

Cassie rubbed the bump beneath her loose-fitting shirt.

Henry Ward had no idea he'd just protected his unborn child, too.

"...," Henry ordered. "There's ...more than one shooter."

# THE DEPUTY'S BABY

## TYLER ANNE SNELL

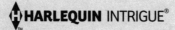

This book is for Marjorie and Annmarie. You two have been by my side, rooting for me since before I could remember. Even now you two are my own personal cheerleaders, and I couldn't ask for anyone better! You might have a dedication in this book but know that you help me write every single one. Love you!

ISBN-13: 978-1-335-52657-1

The Deputy's Baby

Copyright © 2018 by Tyler Anne Snell

Recycling programs for this product may not exist in your area.

**Printed in U.S.A.**

**Tyler Anne Snell** genuinely loves all genres of the written word. However, she's realized that she loves books filled with sexual tension and mysteries a little more than the rest. Her stories have a good dose of both. Tyler lives in Alabama with her same-named husband and their mini "lions." When she isn't reading or writing, she's playing video games and working on her blog, *Almost There*. To follow her shenanigans, visit tylerannesnell.com.

### Books by Tyler Anne Snell

### Harlequin Intrigue

### *The Protectors of Riker County*

*Small-Town Face-Off*
*The Deputy's Witness*
*Forgotten Pieces*
*Loving Baby*
*The Deputy's Baby*

### *Orion Security*

*Private Bodyguard*
*Full Force Fatherhood*
*Be on the Lookout: Bodyguard*
*Suspicious Activities*

*Manhunt*

Visit the Author Profile page at Harlequin.com.

## CAST OF CHARACTERS

*Henry Ward*—After a stint in undercover work ends in tragedy, this new deputy just wants a clean slate. It isn't until there's an attack on the sheriff and he discovers a clue from his past that he realizes simply walking away isn't an option, especially when a woman he spent one amazing night with comes back into his life. And she's pregnant with his child.

*Cassie Gates*—Dispatcher for the sheriff's department, this longtime employee has been through her own set of traumas due to the danger of the job. Yet, after an even more dangerous threat comes to the county and sets its sights on her and her unborn child, she turns to the only person who is just as committed to seeing the madman stopped.

*Calvin Fitzgerald*—Henry's former partner and close friend was killed in an undercover operation years ago yet is somehow connected to the current trouble that's found its way to Riker County.

*Michael*—The mystery man known only by a first name could be the key to figuring out what's going on. If only he can be caught.

*Kristen Gates*—As Cassie's sister and neighbor, she finds herself in the middle of danger when she refuses to leave her baby sister's side.

*Hawk*—Owner and bartender of The Eagle, he's made himself known as a friend to local law enforcement and is more than willing to help them in a pinch.

*Suzy Simmons*—Chief deputy and right-hand woman to the sheriff, she's the one everyone looks to when danger sweeps across the county.

# *Prologue*

"Listen, I need you to buy me a drink."

Henry Ward put his beer bottle back on the bar's top and glanced at the couple next to him. Well, considering what the woman just told the man, he guessed they weren't a couple at all. It was well past the afternoon, but the bar hadn't yet filled up. If he hadn't been so focused on mentally prepping for what he had to do the next day, he probably would have noticed that he and his bar stool companion weren't alone.

"Say what?" the man next to Henry asked. He had a slight slur that sounded like he was trying to talk through a coat of syrup. That wasn't exactly surprising considering Henry had watched him down four very potent drinks within the last hour. Ones that had no color other than dark brown and could be smelled a few feet away. The woman must not have had the chance to catch on to the fumes yet or just hadn't registered the slur. Or maybe she didn't care. Either way, it wasn't his business.

Yet he couldn't help keeping an ear turned to the conversation.

"I need you to pretend that you bought me a drink, I should say," the woman was quick to add. There was some hesitation in her words, but she took the bar stool on the other side of the man, three seats down from Henry.

He glanced over to see the blond of her hair, curled and running down the length of her back, but couldn't get a good angle on her face. He turned his gaze back to the TV over the bar area and fingered the label on his bottle.

"My, uh, sister Kristen just told me she's bringing one of her coworkers over to meet me. She's been trying to set us up for a while now and…well, she won't take no for an answer. So I thought I'd take the option off the table." The woman waited for him to respond. When a moment stretched on, she laid it out simply. "Can I just sit here and talk to you for a few minutes? Maybe throw in some fake laughing every once in a while for show?"

Henry snorted but then covered it up by taking another pull of his beer. Even though he'd been sitting in the Eagle longer than the man a stool over from him had been, he'd only had the one drink. The only reason he'd even left his hotel for the bar was nerves. He had a job interview the next day.

An important one at that.

"Sure thing, hon," the man finally answered. The slur went past the subtle side and right to blatantly obvious. "I'll be your shoulder to lean on *all night long*. You're such a pretty little thing."

Henry glanced over at the two again in time to see the woman's hand, rising to grab the bartender's attention most likely, stall in midair. There was no denying the man between them was drunk now. Henry knew she'd heard it clear as day.

And it had bothered her.

"Oh, you know, *thank you* for that," she hurriedly said, hand already back on the bar's top. "Really. But I just…well, you know I just realized how rude it would be to lie to my sister. I mean, she's a pain, believe me, but I should just be honest with her. So thank you again, but I don't think this was the best idea." She was off the bar stool faster than the drunk man could probably process the movement. "I'm sorry for the interruption. Enjoy the rest of your night!"

"I don't think so, sweetie," the man managed to rasp.

Henry tensed as his neighbor started to turn around.

"You can't just leave me hanging like that. It isn't nice."

Henry was a second away from making the man turn around on his stool, with more than a few stern words, but the woman beat him to the punch. Her voice, sweet as honey moments before, took on a sharp edge.

"If you think I'm not nice, then you wouldn't like my Taser," she said simply.

It did the trick.

The man mumbled and then was facing his empty glass again.

Henry smirked as the woman walked away. He didn't look after her. He didn't need to be doing anything other than worrying about his interview. Though admittedly he wanted the man next to him dealt with. Instead of minding his own business again, he caught the bartender's eye and waved him over. He pointed his thumb at the man now cursing all women beneath his breath.

"I think this one needs a cab called in right about now," Henry said.

The bartender, an older gentlemAn with no hair on his scalp but at least a year's worth of hair on his chin, nodded. Without looking at the man in question, he sighed.

"One's already on the way," he said. "Gary gets pretty foul after four of his drinks. If I don't send him off after that, he won't pay the cabdriver when they get him to his place."

"Good policy," Henry admitted, impressed.

The man named Gary swore at the two of them but nothing that made sense.

"If you get him into the cab so I don't have to, next drink is on the house," the bartender added, annoyance clear in his voice. "I'd rather not deal with him tonight."

Henry felt the now-room-temperature beer between his hands. It would be nice if he had a cold one. "Deal."

He spent the next five minutes or so trying to get Gary to calm down. Even without the woman coming over, Henry would bet Gary could still have managed to get riled up all on his lonesome.

During the last two years, Henry had worked alongside men like Gary, known them like he knew himself. They were angry no matter the drink in their hand or the people at their side. The way they held themselves, the way they dressed, spoke and even held their glasses or bottles showed Henry men who were unhappy and, for whatever reason, wanted to stay that way.

Being around them was more than a job. It was an exercise. One that had worn him down to the point of exhaustion.

Which was why his interview the next day was important.

He needed a new routine.

Gary, however, didn't seem to want anything other than his current mood. He grumbled and cursed as Henry took him to his cab. Henry watched after him for a moment. The night air was cool and apparently rare, according to the manager from his hotel. Henry almost considered going back to his hotel room and trying to get a good night's sleep. But just as quickly, he realized that wasn't going to happen. He had too much on his mind. Not to mention a free beer back inside.

It wasn't until he had that free beer between his hands that a new wave of night air rolled in around a small group of people that Henry thought about the blond woman again.

It might have been a Wednesday, but apparently that

did little to diminish the bar's popularity. Ten or so patrons had eked in and were already either playing pool or sitting around, drinks in hand and conversations going strong. Finding the one person without either was fast work.

Henry wished he'd looked for the woman sooner.

Standing from a booth she'd commandeered in the corner, one of the most beautiful women he'd ever seen was waving at the new group of people who'd just come in. The long, curly blond hair he'd already seen was half pinned back, showing an open face made up of high cheekbones and a long, thin nose. Her lips were rimmed in pink. Even from this distance he could still see the green of her eyes as they moved from who must have been her sister Kristen to a man who must have been her arranged date. Despite what Henry had heard her say about the man, he was impressed to see her expression gave none of her distaste away. Instead she was exuding nothing but enthusiasm and politeness.

It made something in him shift and before he had time to be surprised at himself, Henry did something he wasn't expecting. With one look at the empty second pool table in the corner, he straightened his shirt, ran a hand through his hair and started to walk over to the group. His sights set squarely on the woman with green eyes.

The sister picked him up on her radar the moment he was a few steps away. It didn't stop Henry. He felt a smile pull up his lips and hoped it was pleasant enough.

He also hoped the blonde hadn't already committed to her arranged date. Or else things were about to get awkward.

"Hey, sorry, about that," Henry started, eyes locked on target. "Work called and I had to answer." He motioned back to the pool tables. "But one of the pool tables is open now if you wanted a rematch."

The group turned to him as a whole, but the blonde didn't miss a beat.

She grinned. "If you really want to lose again, then who am I to stop you?"

Henry didn't have to fake the grin that stretched one corner of his lips higher.

"Wait." The sister butted in. For a moment Henry thought the jig was up, but then she laughed. "She actually beat someone at pool?"

Henry shrugged.

"Believe me, I'm not proud about it," he said. "I even owe her a drink because of it. A drink that's past due now."

The woman, once again, didn't skip a beat. "Then let's fix that, shall we?"

She smiled at her sister, said a quick, "Excuse me," and followed Henry to the bar. Without another word between them, she ordered a drink. It wasn't until the group she'd left behind settled into a booth that she spoke.

"I'm assuming you overheard my conversation with

the man at the bar," she said, voice low. It was back to honey.

"I did," he confirmed.

Her smile returned.

"Thanks for helping me out," she said. "In my sister's words, as the baby of the family, I never know what's good for me. She thinks that's Stanley, and I think she has too much time on her hands."

Henry snorted. "My brother plays that age card on me from time to time, too. I know the pain."

The woman laughed.

It was a very attractive sound from a very attractive woman.

"I'm Cassie, by the way. Thanks again for being quick on your feet. You saved my night."

"The name's Henry. And I wouldn't thank me yet." Riding a genuine wave of excitement, he leaned closer, careful to keep out of her personal space but just close enough that he smelled her sweet perfume. He felt the new grin seconds before he heard it in his own voice. "I'm actually *really* great at pool."

## Chapter One

Henry was looking through the passenger's side window at the Eagle, trying to pretend he wasn't thinking of a beautiful woman.

"This is one of three bars in Riker County worth their salt," explained the driver and temporary tour guide, Sheriff Billy Reed. His cowboy hat sat on the center console between them. It was a reminder that Henry was in the Deep South now where cowboy hats could be normal even if cowboys in Alabama were few and far between. "The owner, nicknamed Hawk because nothing gets past him, also runs the bar and does it well. He makes a mean drink and doesn't put up with any nonsense. Also has a memory of steel. Go to him once or twice and he'll know your drink for life. And when to send you off." The sheriff cut a smile. "I suggest you don't force him to do that, though. Getting on his bad side wouldn't be the best thing to do if you want to fit in with our crowd. This is one of local law's favorite haunts."

Henry grinned, deciding not to tell the man he was

sure he'd already met the famous Hawk and seen up close how he operated. Seven months ago he'd been in the bar the day before interviewing for the Riker County Sheriff's Department deputy's position. One he had now held for a week.

The night after the interview he'd left town fast and hadn't been back since. However, Henry was sure he'd been there long enough to peg the man next to him as one of the good ones. Quick to laugh, quick to teach, more pride than most men showed in their entire lives just while staring at one bar within his jurisdiction. It was crystal clear that Sheriff Reed loved his job, his home and the people he had sworn to protect.

The only thing Henry hadn't seen yet was how quick Billy went from fun-loving to business when something serious went down. Sure, Henry had read and seen news stories where the man and his department had been quick on their feet, but he was a man who preferred to deal in firsthand experience. Though, thankfully, no calls that week had been worthy of straining the department, the deputies or its sheriff.

But Henry knew it was only a matter of time.

Bad guys never took breaks for long.

The sheriff took the Tahoe out of Park, backed out of the street-side parking spot and into the two-lane. It was a little after nine in the morning and the small town of Carpenter was mostly sleepy. The Eagle and its surrounding businesses especially, since they catered to the nighttime crowds. Still, Henry kept alert as they drove through, trying to catalog everything he could about Carpenter.

Or maybe he was just trying to keep his focus anywhere but on the bar. Even though he'd only been there once, his thoughts had been sliding back to the place for months. Back to the night when he'd met a woman with honey in her voice and a smile in her eyes.

Back to the night when they had played pool, laughed a lot, and things had been anything *but* sleepy.

A pull of regret momentarily tightened his stomach. He only had one thing to remind him of that night outside of his memories. The small piece of paper tucked into his wallet was a constant reminder of one of the best nights he'd ever had.

And how a man like him shouldn't have anything beyond that.

"Now that we've had a look at where some of the nightlife of Carpenter takes place, I want to show you a few spots of interest during the day," the sheriff said. He paused before continuing and seemed to consider his next words. "Listen, Henry, I know that you're used to fieldwork and that this 'touring the county' thing is probably driving you a little up the wall, but while sitting in a car as I point at stuff might not be exciting, it's hard to serve a county you're flying blind through."

Henry didn't dispute that.

He'd spent the last five years in Tennessee, bouncing around when the job called for it. Not too far a cry from South Alabama but enough of a difference that he couldn't pretend to know the county's flavor just yet.

Henry pulled his mind away from the blond-haired beauty he'd rescued from a blind date, and tried to refocus on the task at hand. This was the first day he'd spent out of the sheriff's department. One of several days to come that he'd spend touring with the sheriff and the chief deputy before getting partnered with another deputy. Then, after a while, Henry would finally get his own cruiser and be able to get back to working alone.

He hoped.

It had been a long time since he'd had a partner, and he wasn't itching to get back into the swing of being one of two.

Sheriff Reed's guided tour took them through the whole of Carpenter, one of three small towns in the county but, according to Reed, they were barely scratching the surface of his hometown.

"Carpenter has been through a lot in the last decade or so. Heck, the *county* has been through a lot," he said later when they pulled into the parking lot of a small diner across the street from the department. Apparently, it was also a law-enforcement favorite, and not just because of its close proximity. "It's made the community stronger, but it's also made the people that make trouble smarter. Trickier. Carpenter, and Riker County as a whole, has a lot of nooks and crannies, country roads and open land, not to mention a good deal of abandoned properties scattered throughout the towns and city, that all make it harder to do our jobs. To keep the community safe, to keep the bad guys from getting the upper hand. Which means we get to work harder and adapt so that never happens."

He put the Tahoe in Park and cut the engine. Henry couldn't help noticing the temperature on the dash read ninety degrees. Though that wasn't counting in the humidity.

Billy glanced at the temperature, too, and smirked. "Which means after lunch I'll start showing you the juicy stuff. Until then you're about to experience one of the best burgers in town and one of the most powerful commercial air conditioners, too."

"And I won't turn that down, either," Henry was quick to say. It wasn't like they were allowed to wear shorts on the job to help fight the heat. Plus, it had been a long time since he'd had a good burger.

They got out of the Tahoe and started across the parking lot. It was summer and the heat kept sticking to its guns. The air was hot and heavy, pressing against his uniform without hesitation. Tennessee had its moments of uncomfortable, but one week in Riker County and he thought he understood the meaning of the word *melting*.

"You weren't kidding about this place being popular with the badges," Henry observed after trying to memorize their surroundings for later. He noted two cruisers at the corner of the building and, if he wasn't mistaken, there was also a personal vehicle of Chief Deputy Suzy Simmons parked in front of the entrance.

"The power of good food in a small town is second to none," the sheriff responded, seemingly not surprised by the turnout. "Though today it's less about the food and more about celebrating." Billy pulled open the door but paused to explain himself over his shoulder. "One of our dispatchers is finally back from an extended vacation. We love all of our department, but I don't think I'm being too sentimental when I say she's close to the heart of it."

Henry had heard that one of the night-shift dispatchers was out of town, but he hadn't thought any more on it. Carpenter might have been a small town, but Riker oversaw two more towns and one city. He hadn't had a chance to meet all the deputies in the department, let alone all the support staff. He hadn't even personally met the dispatchers currently working.

"Plus," the sheriff continued with a smirk, "I may be a man of the law, but I'm not one to turn down a chance at cake."

Henry laughed and followed him inside. It was a small room but efficient. Booths lined the right wall along the windows while a counter stretched across the other with stools in front. In the back corner three booths were filled with deputies, Chief Deputy Simmons, and even one of the detectives, Matt Walker. Some were off duty; others wore their uniforms. All were seemingly in good moods.

Henry spied the half-eaten cake in question sitting in the center of the middle booth, but the woman of the hour wasn't across from it. Even without knowing it was a celebration for her, Henry could have guessed easily enough. Everyone seemed to be leaning in toward her. She stood at the head of the closest table, a gift bag in one hand and tissue paper in the other. Henry couldn't see her face, but he had an uninhibited view of her hair.

It was blond and curly and familiar.

"Deputy Ward," Sheriff Reed announced as soon as they were close enough to the group. Everyone quieted and turned their attention to their leader. Including the woman of the hour. "I'd like to introduce you to our very own Cassie Gates."

Two beautiful green eyes found Henry's and widened.

The woman Henry had spent months trying to forget wasn't just a dispatcher for the department. According to the sheriff, she was the heart of it.

On reflex alone Henry outstretched his hand.

"Nice to meet you," he said. There was a distant tone to his voice. Even he could hear it. Like someone who had just been blindsided. Which, he realized, was exactly what was happening.

Cassie's long lashes blinked a few times but she collected herself quickly.

"Nice to meet you," she repeated. Her tone also sounding dull, hollow.

At least he wasn't the only one who had been caught wholly off guard.

The change in both of their demeanors didn't go unnoticed, either. The sheriff raised an eyebrow. He didn't have time to comment.

The sound of glass shattering filled the air.

And then, right in front of Henry's eyes, the sheriff took a bullet to the stomach.

BETWEEN THE SPACE of two breaths, all hell broke loose in the diner.

Cassie dropped to the floor, a scream caught in her throat. Almost simultaneously the weight of someone else was on top of her, sandwiching her flat against the tiled floor.

Yelling followed by more glass shattering kept the noise levels high and heavy. What was once a celebration had turned into terror. Like a light switch had been flipped, bathing them in a whole new array of shadows. Whoever was covering her tightened around her body, making a cage.

More gunshots sounded overhead. So close, her ears rang in protest. Her colleagues, her *friends*, were returning fire.

Memories of being in a similar situation years before filled her head.

She'd done this before.

She'd been here before. Under fire…

When she thought she was supposed to be safe.

Cassie sucked in a breath, panic thronging her body. If her hands had been free, they would have gone straight to her neck. A gut reaction she'd honed in the last two and a half years. Her fingers would trace the scar at the side of her neck. She'd remember the blood and terror. However, now she couldn't go through that routine. Not when the weight of someone was keeping her to the floor.

So she did the best thing she could. She squeezed her eyes shut and waited.

What felt like an eternity went by until silence finally cut through the madness. It was brief but poignant. As if the diner as a whole had decided to take a collective breath. She couldn't have been the only one whose heart was trying to hammer itself out of her chest.

The body holding her didn't move.

Then, as quickly as the shot had invaded the diner in the first place, the yelling started again. A collective muddled sound where everyone spoke together, canceling one another out with no real progress.

It wasn't until one voice climbed its way above those of the patrons and staff that the chaos was curbed.

"Billy! Billy's down!"

Cassie's personal cage loosened around her enough so that she could look toward Suzy. The chief deputy dropped to her hands and knees next to the sheriff, hands already pressing into the gunshot wound in his stomach. Cassie couldn't look away as blood began to flow onto Suzy's dark hands.

Billy didn't complain about the shot or the pressure.

He didn't even move.

"Are you okay?"

A new voice was at Cassie's ear. The weight on her eased off until a man's concerned expression swam into view. Still, she couldn't look away from the sheriff. She could almost smell the blood.

"Are you okay?" the man repeated. "Cassie?"

Two warm hands came up to cradle her chin. He was gentle as he forced her to look away from the anguishing scene no more than two feet from them. Her boss. Her friend.

"Are you hurt?"

It was like he reached out and slapped her. The shock, the fear, the panic turned analytical. Cassie focused on her body, a new kind of worry coursing through her.

Had they been hurt?

Other than her racing heart, nothing felt different.

"Cassie?"

Clear eyes implored her. She finally recognized them as Henry's. If they had been in any other situation, she would have been fighting a storm of emotions just at the sight of him. Instead she answered him simply. "I think I'm okay."

Henry dropped his hands from her face to her shoulders. He pulled her up but not to her full height. Instead she let herself be led behind the counter that ran the length of the diner. Two waitresses were already huddled there, a reflection of the fear Cassie felt in their faces.

"Stay here," Henry ordered. "There could be more than one shooter."

She nodded and watched as he disappeared. Without his weight keeping her arms down, Cassie was able to reach up and touch the scar on her neck.

Then she dropped her hand to her stomach.

Henry's voice joined the chorus of law enforcement in the diner. It had been so long since she'd heard it like this. Panic and determination. Fear and anger. Uncertainty and planning.

And then here Henry was, among them, adding to the group. It had been over seven months since she'd seen him. Now here he was after no contact whatsoever.

And still he'd tried to protect her.

Cassie rubbed the bump beneath her loose-fitting shirt.

Henry Ward had no idea he'd just protected his unborn child, too.

## Chapter Two

The man who had shot Sheriff Reed had been killed on sight by Chief Deputy Simmons. She hadn't even needed to leave the diner to do it, shooting through the shattered window from next to the booth. Though the man had taken a hit or two from Deputy Dante Mills and Detective Walker in the process.

As for who the shooter was? That wasn't answered until that night inside the department. Suzy, as everyone called her, straightened her back and addressed a room filled to the brim with staff on and off duty. With the sheriff out of commission, she was next in line to lead, and from what Henry had seen of her so far, he more than believed she was ready for the job.

"I just got off the phone with Mara," she began.

Henry knew she was talking about the sheriff's wife. It wasn't a secret how much the man loved his wife and two children. It had been a point of envy for Henry when Billy first talked to him. Now it did nothing but make him feel even more for the man. He knew he wasn't the only one.

"She said that according to the doctor, he isn't out of the woods yet. The bullet missed any vital organs, but he lost a lot of blood."

The woman paused, pain crossing her expression before she could rein it in. Billy had also not kept it a secret that his chief deputy was his best friend and had been for years. They were even godparents to each other's children. He was her family just as the rest of the department was. That closeness was apparent in how the room around Henry seemed to be hanging on her every word.

He couldn't deny he missed that feeling.

Camaraderie that was familial.

"But the doctor also said he's optimistic," she continued. A small smile pulled up the corner of her lips. "And we all know how hard-headed Billy is. Knowing him, he'll be giving out orders by the end of the week from his hospital bed, fussing for his cowboy hat."

There was a chorus of laughter and agreement.

It didn't last long.

Neither did Suzy's smile.

"The reason we're all here is a man named Darrel Connelly," she started again, her tone sharp, serious. A leader addressing those who followed her. "He had no ID on him, but a local police officer recognized him. We ran his name and found that he hadn't been arrested before, but his brother, Tanner, had been for the attempted murder of his girlfriend. Billy's testimony sent Tanner to jail, where he was killed in an inmate-led riot. He was Darrel's only family. So I don't think it would be going out on a limb to say that Billy was targeted out of revenge."

The same group who had laughed in agreement a minute before cursed in unison.

Henry joined in.

"However, until we complete an official investigation, no one in the department will comment to the press. Understood?" Suzy didn't wait for an answer. Instead she took a quick breath and gave a small nod. "While Billy is out, we will continue to do our jobs with the best of our abilities. Any and all questions in the meantime can be addressed to me or Captain Jones. When I know more about Billy's condition, I will update you. Until then, let's continue to make the sheriff proud."

The room's mood swung into a cheer before they started to break up. Suzy stayed up front, talking to those who stopped at her side. Almost like a widow after a funeral. Henry just hoped the analogy didn't come true.

He stayed to the outskirts of the room, hanging back while the bulk of people filtered out. He looked through the crowd, hoping to see the woman he hadn't ever thought he'd see again.

Cassie Gates.

One of Riker County Sheriff's Department's dispatchers.

Henry hadn't even gotten a chance to talk to her

since the diner. After they had secured the area, she'd left with one of the deputies and his wife. She'd been visibly shaken. They all had been, though, if he was being honest.

"Hey, Ward."

Henry turned as Detective Walker came up to his side. He ran a hand through his blond hair and let out a sigh. It was tired.

"Not how you pictured your first week," he commented. It wasn't a question. "Wasn't how I pictured my week, either, to tell the truth."

Henry nodded. "Bad guys don't take breaks for long," he said. "My partner used to say that all the time."

"I hate that it's true but it is." Matt ran another hand through his hair. He'd been the one doing the legwork on Darrel since they got back. Henry imagined he'd have a full, exhausting day tomorrow, too. "One minute we're eating cake and the next—" The detective cut himself off, anger rising to the surface of his expression.

Henry let him have the moment in silence. He took another visible breath to calm himself.

"I just wanted to say thank you for what you did today."

Henry couldn't help his eyebrow rising in question.

The detective elaborated. "You covered Cassie without hesitation," he said simply. "Made sure she was safe before we could get a hold on the situation. Good instincts can't be taught, but they can be thanked."

That surprised Henry. For two different reasons.

One, trying to protect Cassie was a gut reaction. One his body started before his mind could even catch up and act on. He'd heard and seen the shot and then trying to protect her had been his only priority. He hadn't done it for praise or thanks and was surprised he was getting both.

Two, being thanked was strange enough, but being thanked by the detective raised a few questions. The first and loudest was why was Matt invested in her safety? Or, more to the point, was it more personal than colleagues and friends? Did he care more for the woman than the rest?

And why was the mere thought of the two having more than a working relationship bothering Henry so much?

He'd only known Cassie for the one night—and the following morning—and then they'd parted ways. The slip of paper in his wallet was the only connection he'd had to her past then. It was foolish to think she was the same woman. He hadn't seen her in over seven months.

A lot could happen in less time.

Henry shouldn't, and couldn't, be surprised that she might be in a relationship. Heck, *they* hadn't even had one to begin with.

"I was just doing my job," Henry said dutifully, locking down any conflicting emotions that might be splaying across his expression. "Nothing the rest of you wouldn't do in my place. I'm just glad we kept anyone else from getting hurt."

Matt nodded, accepting the statement as true, and started to walk off.

However, Henry couldn't help himself. "I actually wanted to talk to her," he blurted out, surprising himself. "Cassie, that is. I never got the chance at a proper introduction." It was a lie, but Henry wasn't about to admit to the detective that he had already met the woman... At a bar before going back to his hotel room. Especially if the two were involved. "Do you know where she is? I haven't seen her since we left the diner."

Matt's brow furrowed. "She went to the hospital afterward, but now, if I'm not mistaken, she's back at my place. I told her not to bother coming into the department tonight. Technically she doesn't start back until next week."

Henry's gut dropped more than it should have. He had just confirmed the theory that Cassie and Matt were involved. Some of that emotion must have showed in his expression.

Matt gave a small smile. "You know, I'm about to head there myself but need a ride. If you give me a lift, I can trade you a home-cooked meal. I don't think any of us has had anything to eat yet. Plus, I'm sure Cassie will want to thank you for earlier."

The offer felt genuine. Matt hadn't picked up on any of Henry's thoughts.

But even those thoughts gave him little ground to argue with. Though Henry had to admit he didn't like the idea of Cassie with someone else, he knew it was for the better.

People around him got hurt. Plain and simple.

But that didn't stop him from accepting the offer.

He still wanted to see her. If only to make sure she was really okay.

They said goodbye to Suzy, asking again to be kept in the loop, and were on the road to Matt's house within minutes. The detective gave directions, but other than that their conversation was light. Henry wanted to get to know more about him but decided he already knew enough. The lead detective was good at his job, nice to his team and loyal.

He reminded Henry of Calvin, his old partner.

A good man.

*A man that Cassie deserves.*

The thought popped into his head so quickly he couldn't brace himself for it.

How had a woman he'd known for such a short time affected him so much? It made no sense. And was dangerous. Henry needed this job. He needed a new start. Banishing any and all thoughts of Cassie Gates past professionalism wasn't something he wanted. He *needed* it.

*Get a grip on yourself.*

Henry loosened his shoulders, put on a polite smile and was ready when they finally pulled up to the detective's house.

"Home sweet home," Matt said over the hood of the

car when they got out. "I don't know about you, but I'm ready to eat a horse."

The house was a good size with a nice yard. Simple and quaint. Two cars were parked in the driveway. One Henry recognized as the detective's personal vehicle, the other he'd not seen before. Lights were on in the dining room, the curtains open enough that Henry got a clear view of the table.

And Cassie sitting at its end.

She must have felt his stare. She looked out the window and met his eyes.

She didn't smile.

Maybe coming hadn't been a good idea.

"I should also probably warn you," started Matt, walking up the sidewalk that led to his front door. He paused at it, hand on the handle. "You're about to meet a very loud, slightly intrusive woman. I mean, don't get me wrong, I love her, but sometimes she can be a little overpowering when you first get to know her." There was a smile in his voice. "She calls it curiosity."

Henry didn't remember Cassie being loud, certainly not intrusive. At the bar she hadn't kept poking around when he'd said he couldn't talk about his current job and, in fact, hadn't asked too many really personal questions at all. He'd treated her in kind.

Still, he had to remind himself he didn't know her past their one shared night of passion.

That passion.

Even months later his body remembered it. Craved it.

Henry cleared his throat and followed the detective inside. He was just about to agree with his earlier thought that coming had been a bad idea when they made it to the dining room. Cassie was staring up at them. She looked tired. It reminded him that there were more important things than their past. She'd been witness to one of her friends almost dying across from her.

"I invited Henry to join us for dinner," Matt greeted. "Since…well, today didn't go as planned."

Cassie looked between them. It encouraged Henry to respond.

"It's nice to officially meet you," he lied again. If she was with the detective, he didn't want to make anything awkward. Not when Riker County was his chance to start over. He didn't want to make enemies his first week on the job. And judging by the look she was giving him, he could only assume she was trying to figure out what to say herself. The least he could do was try to help her out.

Cassie's green, green eyes widened, but she didn't get a chance to respond. Sound from the other room turned into a flurry of motion that converged on the detective next to him within seconds. Henry tensed, but Matt was laughing into the hair of the woman whose arms were wrapped around him.

"My God, Maggie," he said, reciprocating the embrace. "Ever think about playing football?"

The woman covered his mouth with hers in a quick but strong kiss. She wasn't smiling when she pulled away.

"I'm glad you're okay," she said. "If something had happened to you, I would have hurt you myself."

"Of that I have no doubt." Matt reached up and squeezed her shoulder. He turned to Henry. "This is Maggie Carson. Apparently my linebacker of a fiancée. Maggie, this is our newest deputy I was telling you about. Henry Ward."

Maggie's gaze lifted to his. Her handshake was firm.

"Thanks for bringing him home," she said, sincere. "My car's been acting up and I stole his to pick Cassie up from the hospital."

Henry felt his eyebrow rise. He turned to Cassie. "I thought you said you were okay."

He wouldn't have left her alone otherwise.

She gave him a polite smile, one he'd seen when he first met her at the Eagle, and stood from her seat.

Henry's eyes zipped downward.

Right to Cassie's stomach.

She placed a hand over it, protectively.

"I was," she said. "But I wanted to make sure he was, too."

## *Chapter Three*

"You're pregnant."

It wasn't a question but it wasn't a statement, either. It felt like a confused in-between. Henry Ward had been thrown for a loop and was still trying to find his way back to solid ground. Cassie tried to help, even if she was also looking for some better footing herself.

It wasn't every day that the father of your child appeared out of thin air for the first time since the night he'd spent with you months before, then potentially saved your life and pretended he'd never met you before.

It was all confusing.

"I am," she confirmed, though it wasn't needed. "Seven months, give or take."

Cassie would bet Henry was doing some of the fastest math he'd ever done in his life. All while staring at her pregnant belly. Since she'd never had kids before, she wasn't showing as much, but there was no denying the bump once she brought attention to it.

The man wasn't stupid. If his math was even in the ballpark, he'd guess that he was the father. However, he didn't ask the question. Then again, she didn't think he would. Not after he'd made it clear they didn't know each other.

*You didn't speak up, either*, Cassie pointed out to herself.

The weight of the day erased thoughts of Cassie's personal life for the moment. She moved her hand across her stomach.

"The doc gave the okay, though," she said. If Maggie, the ex-reporter, or Matt noticed anything off about the two of them, they didn't say a word. "But you can never be too careful. Plus, I wanted to be there for Mara."

Henry tore his eyes off her stomach.

"That's good," was all he said.

Matt put a hand on his shoulder and steered the deputy into the kitchen. Cassie settled back into her chair while Maggie followed the men. She was soon back with the dinner they'd just finished making. Nothing too fancy, just something to kill their hunger. Cassie doubted any of them could take any real pleasure from a meal until Billy could, too.

Like her hand had a mind of its own again, it moved up and touched the scar at her neck. Maggie didn't miss it. She took the seat next to Cassie and patted her back.

"You're okay," Maggie whispered. "You *both* are okay. This will all get sorted out. Have faith."

Cassie felt herself nod.

Maggie started a volley of questions as soon as the men were back and seated. More than anything Cassie wanted to pay attention, to learn more about Henry, a man at times she'd wondered if he was even real. Yet there was a rising feeling of overwhelming vulnerability in her chest. It tightened her stomach and pulled out some of the fear and anger she'd felt at the diner.

She didn't know if it was because she was pregnant, because the man she'd spent the last several months hoping would call had showed up, or because she just hadn't had the time to process everything, but suddenly she couldn't just sit there anymore.

"If y'all hadn't have been at my party, this wouldn't have happened," she said, cutting Matt off midsentence.

He was quick to shake his head.

"Cassie, you know as well as I do that you and your party had nothing to do with this," Matt said in defense. "That man was angry, probably out for revenge. Location doesn't deter someone stuck in the mind-set that they're going to try to take on the law."

"But it did give the bastard the opportunity, didn't it?"

She felt the heat that surged through her words seconds before Matt's eyes widened a fraction. She'd bet Maggie's were probably wider, too. It wasn't every day that Cassie Gates had an outburst. She was the sweet one. The Southern girl who always smiled and was agreeable. The one who stayed optimistic when things went badly.

Her cheeks stung now that she'd broken out of her

normal character. It didn't help that Henry was there, staring at her with those eyes of steel. The same eyes that had traced her lips seconds before he'd kissed her for the first time. The same eyes that had traveled across her bare skin sometime later in the night.

Cool, hard steel she hadn't seen since.

And she hated that she was thinking about that night right now. After the day they'd been through, it didn't seem so important.

Yet she could feel the tears of being rejected starting to push themselves forward.

"Cassie…" Maggie began, but her tone was what finally broke the dam that Cassie had put up to keep herself sane after the diner.

The chair scraped against the floor as she pushed herself back and stood. With one hand on her stomach, Cassie met no one's gaze. "Sorry, I'm just tired and hormonal," she declared. "I don't mean to be rude, but I think I'd like to go home now."

Maggie, bless her, must have caught on that Cassie meant what she said.

"Okay," she said, a reassuring smile lifting her expression. "That's fine. Let me at least make you a plate before we go, though, all right? Tired or not, you *two* still need to eat something."

There was force behind her words. A mother mothering a soon-to-be mother. Practically the lifeblood of the South. But she was right.

Cassie nodded and collected her plate. "I'll help."

Without looking at the men, or the one in particular, Cassie fled to the kitchen, a storm of emotions battling it out in her chest.

THE WOMEN WERE out and gone before Henry could think of a reason to pull Cassie aside, alone. Not that it would have changed anything. Cassie could have medaled at the Olympic sport of avoidance with how she'd skirted him on the way out.

Instead of asking her the million-dollar question, he'd been left watching through the dining room window as she slid into Maggie's car.

Not that he blamed her.

He'd just burned any normal bridge they could have had, announcing that he'd never met the woman before in front of her coworkers. Her friends.

Henry resisted the urge to slam his fist down on the tabletop.

Seven months give or take.

That give or take could make the difference.

Had she met someone after him?

Or was he the father?

How had he missed that detail at the diner?

Why had he lied?

And why hadn't Cassie corrected him?

Too many questions and no one to ask them of. At least, not right now.

"I'm sure Billy already told you, but we've been

through a lot as a department the last few years," Matt said, breaking the silence they'd fallen into. He moved his food around on his plate before dropping his fork and taking up his beer. "Stuff that scars. But I guess with your last job you know that better than most of us."

It wasn't a question. Few had been aware of the finite details that went along with his last job. The detective hadn't been one of them, but Henry knew he wasn't stupid. It was public knowledge that his partner, Calvin Fitzgerald, had died during an undercover operation.

Henry took a long pull from his beer as thoughts about Cassie were momentarily replaced by the one part of his past he'd been forced to leave behind.

"Scars are par for the course in this field," he said. "Everyone seems to get them, no matter which side they're on. And even if they aren't on a side at all. A damn shame, if you ask me."

Matt picked up his beer and tapped it against Henry's bottle with a *clink*. "Amen to that." He paused, his bottle hanging in midair. "But some of us have literal scars. Ones that came from calls that were way too close. Cassie's one of them. So I'm sure she's swimming in a sea of bad memories right now. When the dust settles and *when* Billy heals up, you'll see us all in a better light." Matt smirked. "Until then, try not to take any general grumpiness personal."

"Deal."

Henry didn't have the heart to tell the man that any

ill feelings he might get from Cassie were more than deserved.

Instead they finished their dinner just as Maggie returned to help clean up. The way she and the detective moved in tandem without even realizing they were doing it was refreshing to see. The only relationships Henry had been around in the last few years had been dangerous, toxic and unpredictable. Ones that were filled with uncertainty and almost always sank his world into trouble.

Which was why he'd come to Riker County in the first place.

He wasn't looking for redemption and he sure as hell wasn't looking for a second chance at his old life. He didn't want to make things better. That was another bridge that had already burned.

All Henry wanted now was a big heap of nothing.

He wanted a clean slate.

But could he do it? Could he start over? Or had his last job rubbed off on him too much?

Henry sat heavily in the driver's seat of his car after saying 'bye to the couple. He waved at Matt, who retreated into his house, Maggie at his side.

What about Cassie?

And her unborn son?

THE HEAT WAS THICK. Heavy. Unforgiving.

He didn't care.

"What was that?" His voice wasn't low. He was yelling. Again, he didn't care. "You all had one job. *One job!*"

With a flourish he swept his arm over the desk. Everything on its top flew off and crashed to the floor. The man across from him winced. The woman holding his hand did not.

"We saw an opportunity and snapped at it," she hissed, all venom.

"You could have ruined everything," he yelled back. The keyboard that clung to the desktop by its cord didn't last long. He put more feeling into his swing and it, too, crashed to the floor. This time the computer went with it.

The man across from him flinched again like he'd been the one struck. His woman didn't bend.

"We have been waiting for you to put your plan into action for months," she retorted, fire in her words. In a detached sort of way he noticed the tension that had tightened her muscles. He'd bet she was doing everything in her power not to throw her entire body into her anger. Her rage. Under different circumstances he might have been impressed.

At the moment he was not.

"What we're doing, what *I'm* doing, isn't planning some stroll through the park or setting up some simple con," he said, pulling some of his own frustration back into himself. With Darrel's death he'd already lost one of his players. He wasn't willing to lose any more. Not yet. Not when they were so close. He straightened his tie and ran a hand over his hair to smooth it down.

"It isn't a plan at all, really. It's a vision. One that will only work if *we don't do whatever the hell we want to*."

His calm shattered in an instant. He grabbed the lip of his desk and pulled up. If it had been his home office desk, it wouldn't have budged, but this one was cheap. The desk flipped over without much resistance.

Paula was quick. She was up and out of her chair in a flash, long legs graceful in their movement. Her poor excuse for a boyfriend, Jason, wasn't as fast. The weight of the desk pinned the top of his foot. He yelled out in pain.

Again, if it had been his personal desk, Jason's foot would have been broken by the weight.

"Things are about to get crazy," he continued, voice lost to the strain of trying to figure out if he should keep his tantrum going. "And that chaos *is* the goal, the end game." He fixed Paula with a look that kept whatever she was about to say behind her lips. "No more acting out of line in the name of revenge. No more taking shots because you have the opportunity. You're here for more than something so insignificant."

Paula crossed her arms over her chest. She made no move to help Jason free himself. It was as if she'd already forgotten him.

Which was even better.

"What's more significant than revenge?" she asked, cool and calm. "What's better than making the people who wronged us and ours suffer?"

He was quick to answer. "The power to prolong both."

For the first time since he'd summoned them both into his makeshift office, Paula's expression went blank. Then, slowly, she smiled. "Then let's go make some chaos."

## Chapter Four

The night ended without any more fuss. Cassie went home, showered and then took comfort in the arms of her padded duvet. But only after dropping the air-conditioning down a few degrees. She'd had a good pregnancy so far when it came to morning sickness, but she never stopped being amazed at how hot she got.

Her sister Kristen called her a walking furnace.

Cassie lived up to the name the next morning. She woke up sweating. It wasn't until she made it to the kitchen for a glass of water that she fought through the haze of sleep and remembered everything that had happened the day before.

She downed half the glass and went in search of her cell phone. It had also spent the night tangled in the bedsheets. Which meant her battery hadn't been charged. A notification showed it was less than 15 percent. The one below it listed two new text messages. Cassie perched on the side of the bed. She didn't give herself time to worry about what each message said before opening and reading both.

The first was from Denise, the Caller ID reading Mrs. Beadle. Several hearts were on either side of the name. Cassie smiled. Her eldest sister and sibling was just as maternal as their mother. She'd actually been the first person Cassie had called after getting to the hospital to make sure everything was okay with the baby.

Which hadn't made Kristen happy, since she was local and Denise lived in Colorado. However, it was a force of habit to call the eldest Gates sibling and had been since she'd moved out of the house when they were younger. Denise had a gift for worrying about a person with all of her being while simultaneously helping comfort that same person with all of her being. And that was what Cassie had desperately wanted. Comfort, released of the fear and uncertainty that had just crashed back into her life. Both sisters said in their own ways to call them when she was up and moving around.

Cassie sighed.

It was only a matter of time before word got out to the rest of the Gates clan. Then her brothers would be the ones filling her inbox.

It came with the territory of being the youngest of six siblings. The baby. Which, by default, meant she received the full weight of their worry and less and less of their confidence. Never mind Cassie was twenty-nine, had a mortgage and was a few months shy of becoming a full-fledged mother.

She placed a hand on her swollen belly.

A love she didn't think was possible consumed her

entire heart and soul at the touch. Relief cascaded down until she felt like crying.

The sound of gunfire shot across her thoughts.

If anything had happened to her son at the diner…

Cassie fisted the sheets in her hands, suddenly as angry as a kicked hornet's nest.

Then she was picturing gray eyes and feeling the warmth of a body protecting hers.

Henry. Henry Ward.

The rage at the most horrific what-if about her son lessened into a different kind of anger. One that, if she was being honest, was backed up by insecurity.

After a night of connection so deep with the man that it had surprised her, he had promised to call when he got back home.

Yet he never had.

No call. No text. No anything.

What's more?

He'd told her his name was Henry Smith.

How idiotic she found that now. Of course the gorgeous man she'd had a wonderful night of passion with after meeting in a bar had given her a fake name. She should have taken it as a hint he didn't want to see her again after he'd told her he couldn't give his number out because he didn't have one yet. But, boy, if she hadn't believed him then. Hung on his every word.

She had been a sheep, like normal. He, a lion.

Embarrassment began to burn in Cassie's cheeks. She shook her head.

"Nothing's changed," she said out loud, stern with herself. "You have this baby and this baby has you. You don't need strangers who lie. No matter how sexy that stranger is." She patted her stomach. "You can do this, baby mama."

It was a good little talk that mostly did the trick.

She went around the house trying her best to get back into any semblance of a routine. She ate, she cleaned and she cooked, all while making calls to her family and friends. The former she assured she was okay, the latter she asked for updates on the sheriff. Maggie was the only person she could get hold of who knew anything substantial about Billy's condition. He was stable but still unconscious. Once he did wake they'd be able to go from there. It was good news, all things considered, yet it wasn't enough to erase the fear that had taken root.

It wasn't until she finished strapping a pan covered in aluminum foil into the passenger seat of her car that Cassie realized she was going to try to help alleviate some of that stress for her friends by delivering a platter of lasagna to the department. Just in time for lunch like the Southern woman her mother taught her to be. Sure, it wasn't a normal lunch meal, but she blamed that on the baby in her stomach. She'd been craving cheese and tomato sauce for days. Two birds, one stone.

The dish didn't budge as she drove to the heart of Carpenter. Since she was alone she said a few curses under her breath about the weather. Furnace or not, their South Alabama town was just plain old miserable. A blanket heat, a choking humidity and a baby in her belly were not complimentary details that made the situation better. By the time she pulled into the parking lot at the sheriff's department, she was ready to sprint inside for the lobby air conditioner if she had to.

The day shift had most of the lot filled, but Cassie couldn't help noticing a car she didn't recognize. Which probably belonged to Henry, she realized.

The father of her child.

No amount of lasagna or air-conditioning was going to smooth over that particular stress. Despite her feelings, reservations and insecurities, she couldn't sidestep the man forever. Especially if he was a deputy.

That meant that she was going to have to decide sooner or later if she was going to tell him the truth.

Guilt pooled in her stomach, but she was quick to combat it with the facts.

As much as she wanted to believe that the man she'd had a connection with months ago was great, she couldn't escape the reality that he had lied to her about his name and then disappeared completely from her life.

He had been a one-night stand, albeit a great one. That was what it boiled down to.

*One* night.

That didn't seem like a lot when contemplating letting him possibly have a place in her unborn child's life.

Cassie cut the engine and patted her stomach.

"No matter what, it's going to be all right," she told her son, though she knew it was more to herself. With a sigh that she was sure even he felt, Cassie got out of the car and pushed into the heat.

She wasn't two steps behind her car when her plan of action to escape the heat was halted.

"Excuse me."

Cassie turned in time to watch a man walk out from between two of the cars. He immediately held his hands up in defense and pointed behind him.

"I was on the way over here from the coffee shop," he explained. "Now I realize how creepy it must look, me just popping out from the back of the parking lot."

The man managed to look sheepish. He was well dressed, she guessed in his early thirties, and had a shock of dark red hair that was trimmed neat to the scalp. Cassie had never seen him before, but nothing about him screamed hostile. The smile left behind from his laughter put her at ease.

"I assume you work at the department?" This time he motioned to the building behind her.

She'd been with the sheriff's department for years and knew it like the back of her hand. It stood between the county courthouse and the local television station, a two-story wrapped in faded orange brick and concrete. It was wider than its neighboring buildings but shorter. The second floor was vacant minus a room used for storage. Still, the department had spent years cultivating efficiency in the first floor's space. Cassie was particularly proud of her dispatcher's area.

"Yes, I do," she answered, mimicking his smile.

"Though at the moment I'm off duty. But I'd be glad to try to help you."

"I really do appreciate that, but I'm afraid I have a bit of a weird request." He pulled a plastic sandwich bag from his pocket and held it out to her. There was something inside it. A ring. "Sheriff Reed made a stop into the Carter Home yesterday and a deputy who was with him left this behind."

Cassie took the bag, her heartbeat already quickening.

"I never caught his name, so I figured I'd just bring it in and let you all sort it. Maybe you could return it to its owner?"

Cassie might not have been back at work, but she'd learned of Billy's intended tours for new recruits. In this case, that meant Henry. Which meant fate was having a good ole laugh at her right now. It looked like she'd have to talk to the man sooner rather than later.

"Of course I will. I even know the deputy in question," she answered. "Why don't you come in with me? I'm sure he'd be grateful for you returning this." Maybe she could use the man as a buffer until she decided what to do.

The man shook his head. "I'm actually in a hurry." Again he motioned to the building that butted up to the back of the parking lot. It was a strip mall that housed several businesses, including the best coffeehouse in town. "Would you mind giving it to him instead? I have a friend waiting for me plus a cup of coffee with my name on it."

Cassie was nothing if not accommodating. "I can do that. No problem." She readjusted her purse. Sweat was already forming above her brow. "Can I give him your name so he can at least know who to thank later if the occasion arises?"

"Michael." He held up his hands again, an apologetic look across his face. "I really have to go now. I hope you have yourself a great day."

Before Cassie could press for a last name, he turned, effectively ending their conversation.

Maybe she wasn't the only one in a hurry to get out of the heat.

"IT'S NOT IDEAL." Suzy's mouth tightened. "But it's what I'm saying."

Henry looked across the top of the woman's desk and was trying his best not to look petulant. He knew a very bad thing had happened the day before, but he didn't want to get benched because of it. Not when he'd done nothing but key himself up with thoughts about his future in Riker County the night before. He knew change was inevitable, but that didn't mean he had expected it to start so quickly after joining the department.

"Listen, I get it, I really do," he returned, trying. "I'm the new guy. It only makes sense that the sheriff's case takes precedence over taking me around town and explaining the lay of the land. But isn't there some way I can speed the process up? Maybe have someone write down the places I need to know and I can go when I'm off duty?"

Suzy gave him a flat stare. She looked as tired as he felt. "The idea was to pair you with people who have grown up in the various towns and city in Riker County. It's a process Billy started up when he was elected sheriff and one that I truly believe has helped every new addition to the team. Even support staff has been paired with one of us or a senior deputy to learn, as you said, 'the lay of the land.'" She pointed to herself. "Billy and I were your guides along with Deputy Mills, but now... Well, now plans and priorities have shifted, and as much as I hate it for you, you're going to be sitting at your desk until all the dust settles."

Henry didn't like that. Not one bit. Billy might have stabilized, but regardless of his condition he wouldn't be back to work for months. Which meant Suzy would hold the title of acting sheriff until then. Which meant there might be some shifting around of the deputies, picking up the things that might fall through the cracks of a sudden management shift.

Which meant he might be saddled to his desk a lot longer than he wanted.

"What about Cassie?" The words left his mouth out of desperation. It wasn't until he saw them register in Suzy's face that he himself wasn't keen on the idea. Still, desperation bred desperation. He pushed on. "She's not due back to work until next week, right?

Maybe she wouldn't mind showing me around, all things considered. I heard she grew up in the county."

Henry wasn't about to say he'd heard that from the woman herself, months ago and in between the sheets at his hotel room. The bottom line was that he'd made a point. One Suzy seemed to be considering.

"She spent a few years in Darby, but yeah, the bulk of her childhood wasn't spent too far from where Billy and I grew up." Suzy made a pyramid with her fingers, then tapped two of them together in thought. "Truth be told, I would like to get you out into the field sooner rather than later. I know Billy probably already told you this, but you've got an impressive résumé. I'd rather you use your skills out there trying to keep the county safe than stuck behind a desk."

Henry felt a stab of guilt in his gut. He was proud of his career, sure, but in his mind that career had all but died when his partner had. Being praised for any of it now felt wrong. It hadn't mattered how good he was at reading people, how fast his reflexes were, and how good a shot he could be, at the end of the day, none of it had saved his friend.

And if he couldn't save Calvin, what made any of them think he could save anyone else?

That thought scorched across his mind so quickly he nearly stood from his seat to distance himself from it. Doubting his role as a deputy would *definitely* get someone hurt. Even him.

No. He needed to be ready for anything.

That included Cassie Gates.

"Let me give her a call and feel it out," Suzy declared with a nod. She grabbed the phone but paused before picking it up. "But if she isn't up for it, you'll go to a desk until we can find someone else. Understood?"

There was no malice or annoyance in the woman's tone. Just a boss needing to make sure her charge was on the same page.

And he was.

"I won't push the issue," he said. "Scout's honor."

She smirked at that and dialed Cassie's number without another word. Henry was wondering if he should leave the room when a song started to play out in the hallway. They both looked to the open office door as the song got closer.

"You rang?" Cassie said, popping her head into the room, surprising them both. At seeing Henry there, she faltered but finished her thought. "Or are ringing, I should say." She held up her phone as Suzy hung up hers.

"You're here? Is everything all right?"

Cassie nodded hurriedly. "Yeah, I just thought I'd bring in some lunch for everyone." Her cheeks reddened a little. She groaned. "Which I left in the car. Because pregnancy brain is real." Her eyes flitted to Henry's. Instead of looking away, she held his stare. "I was also distracted by someone in the parking lot looking for you."

"For me?" Henry asked, once again surprised. Outside of the people who worked in the department, he'd made no friends in Riker County. He didn't even know if he could give the people he worked with that title yet. Not to mention no one from his life in Tennessee even knew where he'd gone. At least, no one who would have bothered to visit. And surely if it had been his brother he would have called. "Who was it?"

Cassie pulled a plastic bag from her purse and passed it over. "His name was Michael. He was at the Carter Home yesterday when you came by with Billy. He didn't know your name but knew you were the new deputy." She shrugged. "He was in a hurry, so I said I'd make sure you got it."

There was curiosity in her voice. Henry heard it plain as day. Yet it paled in comparison to his own.

He looked at the bag between his fingers. He didn't open it. He'd recognize the ring anywhere. A warmth that had no business belonging to him started to spread in his memory. Just as quickly it turned ice cold. He looked back to Cassie. If her expression was any indication, she'd caught on to the unwelcome change in his demeanor. Apparently she wasn't the only one.

"Deputy," Suzy said, breaking their stare, "what's wrong?"

Henry met his boss with an even look that he hoped gave nothing away but the facts. He held up the bag. "The last time I saw this ring was a year ago." That cold feeling began to spread as he took a moment before finishing. "It belonged to Calvin Fitzgerald."

By the change in *her* demeanor, Henry knew Suzy recognized the name. And why it was significant.

"A year ago…" she said, fishing.

Henry took the bait.

"The day of the fire," he offered. "The day he died."

## Chapter Five

Henry and Suzy went out to the parking lot in search of Michael but found no one. Cassie went to look at the security footage that covered the lot and had a deputy pause the tape for them until they came back.

"Do you recognize him?" Suzy asked. Thanks to budget cuts, the footage wasn't grade A, but it was enough to make out the key features of the man Cassie had talked to. Red hair, general build and well dressed.

Henry took a moment but shook his head. "No. I don't. Not from Tennessee and not from yesterday, either. If he was at the Carter Home, I didn't see him."

"And you're sure that's the same ring?"

There was a noticeable pause. Cassie glanced over at Henry. He didn't look at the bag or the ring inside.

"There's a chance it could be a different one." Henry met Cassie's gaze and looked away just as quickly. "Maybe this Michael guy was mistaken about who dropped it. I can go after my shift to try to talk to him."

Suzy had opened her mouth to, Cassie assumed,

question the shift in certainty when Detective Ryan Ansler moved into the doorway. His brow was drawn tight.

"Matt needs to see you," was all he said. Though his tone added an understood "as soon as possible" to the end. It rallied Suzy instantly.

"I'm coming. Deputy Ward, keep me updated on what you find out about the ring." She turned to Cassie. "And, Cassie, I have a favor to ask of you. Could you walk with me?"

Cassie nodded without another look at Henry. Part of her wanted to avoid him so she didn't have to worry about their past, present or future just yet. Another part wanted to ask him why he had just lied to Suzy. Because she had no doubt that was exactly what he'd done.

Turned out that other part of her was about to get the chance. Not only did Suzy want her to help show Henry around the county, she wanted her to start today.

"But I can't make you do it," Suzy reminded her as they hovered outside the conference room door. Cassie could see Matt and Captain Jones talking inside, heads bent toward each other, clearly concerned. It put an ounce more urgency in Cassie's gut. "This is strictly a favor. One I'll understand if you turn down."

Cassie couldn't believe herself as she nodded. "The department is under a lot of stress right now," she reasoned, more for herself than for Suzy. "I was on vacation for too long. I'm ready to help out now."

Suzy gave her a smile. It was fleeting after she

glanced at the men in the room. Her shoulders pushed back even more. She gave a curt nod. "Thanks, Cass."

And then Cassie was alone in the hallway.

She contemplated staying there for a while or maybe finding a place to hide from the responsibility she'd just accepted. Or, rather, the man she'd just agreed to saddle herself with. Instead she patted her stomach and walked back to the bull pen to find Henry at his desk.

He looked surprised to see her. So much so, it almost was offensive.

"I'm ready when you are," she greeted, trying to stay as friendly as she normally was. And no more or less than that. If she was going to work with Henry Ward, she might as well embrace it. "We can take my car, since you don't have a cruiser yet. If that's okay with you."

Henry looked like he was about to say something but thought better of it.

"Sounds good to me," he said, standing. He scooped up the plastic bag with the ring and slipped it into his pocket. Then that smile was back. The one that had wholly captivated Cassie months before. The one that had pulled her from an almost-blind date and convinced her to play pool for hours with a man she didn't know.

The one that had led her back to his bed.

A warmth began to move up Cassie's neck to her cheeks. She turned on her heel to try to hide the blush, resigned not to speak to him again until she had better control. However, two steps out the front door and into the heat, she couldn't help herself.

"You lied to Suzy," she accused, still sure in her words. "Why?"

She felt his gaze turn completely on her as he fell into step next to her.

"What do you mean?"

"You said there was a chance that the ring wasn't Calvin's." She spelled out her thoughts. "But you lied. You're positive it is. Why tell Suzy differently? And how are you so sure?"

She turned to the man now. Cassie knew he was good at reading people, one of the few things she *did* know about him. She wanted him to see she wasn't backing down.

Cool gray eyes searched her expression. Two unbelievably soft lips turned up into a small smile. If she hadn't been walking for two, her knees might have decided to give out because of it.

"We haven't seen each other in months and now we're essentially partnered up to tour the county we both work for and the first thing you say when we're alone is that I'm lying." He said the last part deadpan. It wasn't a denial. "I didn't think this was how any of our conversations would start."

"There's a lot of things I'd like to say instead," she admitted, growing hot in temper and not because of former steamy memories. "But this is important. I've learned through years of being here that if the past reaches out to you, then sometimes bad, bad things follow. I'd like to *not* be blindsided twice in two days.

That goes double for the department. What happened to Billy…" She shook her head. "I'd just rather be prepared."

Henry sobered. They were halfway through the side guest parking lot before he answered.

Cassie could feel the sweat already trying to form down her back.

"I know this ring because it used to be mine. I'd know it anywhere, anytime. But after I gave it to Calvin, I never expected to see it again."

"Because he died?" Cassie felt regret at not spending the morning learning more about the man next to her. Now that she had a real last name, she could have at the very least searched the internet for information. She had no idea who Calvin was, why he died, or anything else about Henry before yesterday. Instead of the last puzzle piece being just out of her reach, she felt like she was left holding only one while the rest of the picture was gone. It wasn't a good feeling.

Henry nodded. "Yeah, he died. And his body was never recovered."

Cassie could almost hear him going tight-lipped. It was difficult to talk about.

"And who was Calvin to you?" She had to ask. She omitted the once again obvious fact that she didn't know anything about his past.

Henry kept his gaze straight ahead. "We worked together in Tennessee."

Cassie was given the distinct impression that Henry

sidestepped the rest of the details on purpose but didn't get the chance to say so. They came to a stop at thc back of her car, but not before movement on the sidewalk between the strip mall behind the department parking lot and them caught her eye.

"Hey," Cassie yelled. "That's the guy!"

Henry followed her stare to the red-haired man who had given her the ring in the first place. The man was leaning against the building but pushed himself off it at their attention. He was smiling.

"He's the one that gave me the ring," she added to make sure Henry understood. "Michael."

The deputy didn't need to be told three times.

"Wait here," he said, touching the small of her back on the way around her car. The unexpected contact sent her thoughts scattering long enough that she was slow on registering what happened next.

"Hey, you," Henry called out. "Could we talk for a—"

Michael turned tail and followed the sidewalk through the strip mall and out of sight faster than Henry could finish his sentence. The deputy didn't hesitate in following. His heavy shoes hitting the concrete echoed around the back of the parking lot. Then he was out of sight.

HE WAS FAST. Too fast.

What started as a few yards between them stretched to an even wider gap as Henry followed the sidewalk to the front of the strip mall. Michael used the open space to really lean into his pace. He weaved around a few pedestrians coming out of the coffee shop and then ducked around a well-dressed group going into an office farther down.

Michael might have been fast, but that didn't mean he was going to lose Henry. What he'd lost in a lead, he'd make up for with his stamina. And the way Michael was running, there weren't many places to hide or fully escape without being seen.

Henry might not be familiar with Riker County, but he'd at least figured out the few blocks surrounding the department. The one they were on housed a handful of offices and shops before turning into side streets that led one of two ways, back to the main street in front of the department or to the civic center and several streets that led to downtown. The way the man named Michael was running, he was about to make the decision of where he wanted to go. Either direction, he'd still have to cover a lot of ground to lose Henry.

Or maybe not.

Michael ran across the street, taking a right toward the civic center and downtown. Henry followed suit but had to hit his brakes as a driver refused to hit his. He resisted the urge to bang his fists on the hood as the car drove past. He just wanted to talk to Michael.

Why was he running?

What did he know?

Henry cursed beneath his breath and kicked it back

into high gear. By the time he was across the street and following the sidewalk up and right around a tall building that housed a small office complex, the man had once again spread the distance between them.

However, he stopped before Henry could eat any more of it up. Chest heaving but in no way hesitating, Michael opened the passenger's side door of a car stopped by the curb.

He paused, but only long enough to give a parting speech. The mystery man met Henry's gaze with a wave of his hand.

"Find me if you can," he yelled.

The door shut and the car was pulling away from the curb before Henry could catch up. Adrenaline was coursing through his blood as he skidded to a stop at the curb. The excitement of the chase was making it almost impossible to stop his muscles from readying to keep going. There was no way he could catch the car on foot. And even if he did go back for his car, they would probably already be long gone by the time he made it back.

"Son of a—"

"Get in!"

Henry turned on his heel to see a car stopped a few feet behind him. Not just any car, it was Cassie's. A cloud of curly blond hair stuck out the window as she eyed him.

"Come on," she called. "Get in or we're going to lose them!"

Like she had trained his body by simple command,

Henry wasted no time in jumping into the passenger seat, careful to keep his eye on the fleeing car. It was at the end of the street now, executing a left turn. If they didn't hurry—

No sooner had he had the thought and was inside the car than Cassie hit the gas. The tires actually squealed.

However, Henry's focus abruptly changed directions.

"What *is* this?" he yelled, feeling something warm and soft against the seat of his jeans.

Cassie whipped her car around a stopped truck, dipping into the empty oncoming traffic lane before coming back.

"What?" she shouted back, volume level matching.

Henry reached down as whatever was beneath him shifted.

"Cassie, what am I sitting in?" he asked, voice higher than normal. "It's *warm*!"

"Oh, no, Ms. Moye!"

*"Ms. Moye?"* Henry jumped up and reached down in an awkward attempt to rid himself of the unsettling sensation seeping into the seat of his jeans. His hand hit a hard container. For one wild moment he imagined some kind of urn. When his hand hit foil and then something red, he almost left the car altogether.

"My neighbor Chelsea's lasagna!" She turned the wheel to follow down the street to the left. It put Henry off balance even more. The mushy sensation against his backside became even more pronounced.

"Well, I made it, but it's her recipe. I brought it to the

department for lunch but forgot about it because, again, pregnancy brain is real." She glanced over. "I guess I forgot it was there again. Sorry!"

Henry finally managed a glance down. Sure enough, he'd sat right in a food dish. The aluminum foil had saved some of the lasagna from spilling out, but not all of it.

"I hope you like lasagna with your car, because I'm getting it everywhere," he muttered, pulling the dish out from under him and putting it on the floorboard.

"I need to get it detailed anyways," she said dismissively. Her tone had an edge to it. Concentrated. It reminded Henry of what they were doing.

He adjusted his gaze out the windshield and forgot all about his backside covered in lunch.

"There are no plates on the car," he noted. "I don't recognize it, either. And, again, I didn't recognize the man. There should be no reason he's running. Or, at least, I don't know one."

Henry brought out his phone and started to dial the department.

"Well, for men you don't know, they sure seem intent on losing us." Cassie had to slow as the few cars between them and the black one got caught in a construction zone. "If you're calling this in, let Myra know that we're headed toward the civic center. Wait. Scratch that."

Henry looked up in time to watch the car in question hook a right.

"Where does that street lead?" There was hesitation in her answer, yet Cassie didn't stop her pursuit. "Cassie?"

"That's Keller Avenue," she answered.

He glanced over to see her brows pinched in thought.

"Old houses, an auto shop and then a whole lot of nothing. A weird place to go if you're trying to lose someone following you. It would be easier to lose us in lunchtime traffic near the civic center or downtown."

At her words, or maybe the way she said it, Henry's gut started to yell. But he kept quiet.

The last time he'd listened to his gut, Calvin had died.

He wasn't about to make the same mistake again.

## Chapter Six

There were three cars, two trucks and one tractor driving along Keller Avenue. Cassie maneuvered around each with caution and speed. One of the cars honked at her. The man driving the tractor shook his fist. She didn't care. She was in the zone, tunnel-visioned on the black car in the lead. Soon it would take the bend of Keller and disappear from view if she fell any more behind.

Either way, she wasn't stopping.

It was a surprising sensation. One as a dispatcher she rarely dealt with. Sure, she'd had calls and incidents where all hell felt like it was breaking loose, but typically that was on the other end of the line or radio. In those times she had to be the calm one. Steel in her voice and concentration that rivaled that of the best of the best deputies in her department. It was easy to do when sitting behind a desk. However, now that she was operating on more than just a hint of urgency, she was surprised that she not only wanted to catch the man and get answers, but felt like she needed them.

Maybe it was just her picking up on Henry's desire to know what was going on. Maybe she subconsciously thought it would make her feel better about her current uncertain situation with the man sitting next to her if he at least found what he was looking for.

Or maybe it was just pregnancy hormones craving something other than salty-sweet.

"What does this road turn into?" Henry asked, re-adjusting himself in her periphery. He seemed to still be distracted by the lasagna he was now wearing. He opened up the glove box without permission but was rewarded with a handful of napkins she kept in it just in case.

"It can turn into a county road that runs to the city of Kipsy or, if they take the next turn, they go into an old neighborhood called Westbridge." She thought for a moment. "And, honestly, either option won't be fast. It's a mostly straight two-lane to Kipsy and the neigh-borhood isn't small, but it all leads into a dead end with no other exit. Whoever Michael and his driver are, they aren't making the most progressive choices if they're trying to run away."

Cassie kept on the gas. If she couldn't lessen the gap, then she was determined to at least be close enough to see which choice they were going to make. She hated to admit it, but their black four-door was faster than her older Honda. She'd had the car since she'd moved out of her parents' house. It wasn't meant for high-speed chases. In its old age it was barely meant for normal-speed anything. Getting a new ride had been on her to-do list since she'd found out she was pregnant. Though she might not have a choice than to go car shopping after this episode. There was a slight rattling in her dash, but she couldn't decide if it was any different than the random sounds that came with the car's age.

"The opening to the neighborhood is right after this bend." Layers of trees blocked her from seeing anything other than the road right in front of them. She sat straighter as she turned with the road.

"If they do go into the neighborhood, I don't want you to follow."

That caught her off guard.

"Wait, why not?" she asked, indignant.

Henry's voice was calm but authoritative when he responded. "When people run like this, they usually have a good reason they don't want to get caught. Or, at least, it's a good reason in their own minds."

Cassie glanced over long enough to see his jaw harden.

"And I have a feeling that this Michael wants me to catch him *and* get away at the same time. Which makes him even more unpredictable. So, no, I'm not about to ask a pregnant woman to drive headfirst into what could be a trap."

Henry didn't know it yet but he'd just had the misfortune of walking right into a wall of hormonal anger from said pregnant woman. Cassie's face heated like someone had just turned up her personal oven burner.

"Well, good thing you don't have control over this pregnant woman, Deputy *Ward*," she shot back.

"Cassie, that's not what I meant," he started, too oblivious or too smart to touch on the fact that she'd just put a nasty amount of emphasis on his name. A name that was different from the one he'd given her. "It's just that—"

However, Cassie wasn't having it. Her internal burner was on high. "You think you can just walk back into town after absolutely no contact and then have some kind of hold over me because we spent *one* night together. My being pregnant or not, that doesn't give you the right to decide what I should or shouldn't do!" The bend was finally evening out. Cassie's anger was not. She almost missed the one glaring detail ahead of her on the street. Or rather, the lack of one.

"They must have gone into the neighborhood," Henry said, staring out the window at the empty street.

There was no time to comment on her outburst, Cassie knew, but still couldn't deny she felt a sting at his not acknowledging that he hadn't reached out to her once in the last several months.

"And we're not following," she intoned instead of continuing her rant.

Henry nodded.

He motioned to the shoulder of the street across from the Westbridge neighborhood sign. Cassie put on her flashers and pulled off onto the dirt, angling the car so if they needed to she could floor it right back onto the street. More trees stretched a few feet to their left, closing in the shoulder, while the neighborhood across the street looked like it was being swallowed by them. That was the beauty of Southern Alabama. Not only did you get farms and fields; there were the occasional woods thrown in, too.

"So what? We wait until they come out?" Cassie put the car in park but kept her gaze on the entrance to Westbridge. "What if they don't? What if they go into a house or ditch their car and run through the trees? I think there's a county road that runs parallel to this one they could get to. Or maybe—"

Henry opened the door. The sudden sound made her jump. "Wait, what are you doing? You said we weren't going in there!"

Henry didn't answer until the door was shut and he had walked around to hers. Cassie rolled down the window. The heat pushed against her face. It didn't improve her mood.

"Call the chief deputy sheriff and let her know what's going on. Tell her we followed that same man who gave you the ring earlier."

"And what about you?" Cassie asked, already feeling disgruntled at his show of authority. She'd been with the sheriff's department for years. *He* was the new one. "I thought we weren't going in there."

Then Henry did that thing he had done all those months ago that spelled trouble for Cassie. With a capital T.

He smirked.

It was like his lips were connected all over her body. In her stomach she felt the warmth of memory across her chest, the pain of longing beneath her waist and the irrational fear of being left again by a man she didn't know. Combined, it made for a distraction wide enough to hide the man's motive until he had to spell it out for her.

"You aren't going in there," he said. "But I am."

AT FIRST GLANCE, the neighborhood of Westbridge seemed normal enough. Henry kept his hand on the butt of his service weapon, touched his deputy's badge to re-affirm his decision to follow the lead past the entrance sign, and stalked cautiously past the third house before he understood that his earlier assumption was wrong.

Westbridge was quiet.

Sure, it was a weekday and not yet time for the normal working class to be home, but still it was *way too quiet*. The type of silence that wasn't intentional. No. It was the product of abandonment. Cassie had said the neighborhood was old.

What she hadn't said was that it was a relative ghost town.

One- and two-story houses, some with siding covered in mildew and others in faded brick, sat sentry on either side of Henry as he moved deeper inward.

The driving force of curiosity started to cool in his chest thanks to the nearly overpowering yell of his gut.

*This has to be a trap*, it said.

*But for what? And why?* the less rational part of his mind answered.

All the while both parts focused on the real reason he had rushed headlong into a situation he normally wouldn't have.

The ring.

It shouldn't have been in Riker County.

It shouldn't have been in Alabama.

It *definitely* shouldn't have been in his pocket.

Yet there it was. Like a weight was tied to it, dragging every part of Henry down.

He didn't want to find answers just to satiate his innate curiosity that came with the territory of being in law enforcement.

No. He'd sure as hell earned them.

The road curved enough so Henry couldn't see if the car they'd been following was farther up ahead. Though, by Cassie's estimation, Michael and his mystery driver weren't going to be able to just drive out using another outlet out back. So, instead of staying in the open on the sidewalk, Henry moved across the side yard, deciding to stick closer to the houses to stay more hidden.

Thunder rumbled in the distance.

It should have been a sign. One that foreshadowed the result of Henry's careless decision to pursue the unknown the way he had. Because he knew that was what it was. Carelessness. No backup. No real plan. Just a man hell-bent on understanding why the ring he'd given his best friend was now with him.

But Henry's steps never faltered.

The moment his boots touched the backyard's overgrown grass, he was staring at a man no more than twenty feet from him.

It was Michael. And he had his head thrown back in laughter. Henry took out his gun. It didn't faze the man.

"You know, out of all the houses and backyards, you chose to come into *this* one," Michael said, composing himself. His laughter died away but his grin did not. "I'd heard that you had a set of instincts that bordered on unnatural, but to see it in person? Well, that's a treat."

Henry took in the yard around them as quickly as he could. Tall grass, a privacy fence in disrepair, the side opposite him missing altogether and showing the next yard over. And, as far as Henry could tell, no one else was in the vicinity.

Where was the driver?

"Who are you?" Henry demanded. He pulled up his gun, aiming for the man. Lacking backup wasn't going to stop him from protecting himself if everything went south.

"I'm Michael," he said as if that explained it all.

"Why give me some random ring?" Henry asked. "And then run off?"

Michael was the sole recipient of a joke Henry couldn't even guess at. He racked his brain, flipping through a mental Rolodex of names and faces from what felt like his former life, trying to place the man once again. Yet he was coming up empty. Not a feeling he was used to.

Or liked.

"Trying to find the right answers by asking the wrong questions is an interesting, risky tactic," the man drawled. "One that I'm sure has worked on common criminals and those with less than average IQs, *but* here's the deal, Deputy Henry Ward." He moved his arms wide and smiled to match. "I'm not a criminal. I'm a broker. A smart one at that, too."

Henry had almost had enough of the man. He took a step forward, gun staying on target.

"A broker, huh?" He smirked. Just because he was focused didn't mean he couldn't also show some of the cockiness the mystery man was exuding. "That's a new one. What do you deal in? Let me guess… The cliché answer would be, what, information?"

A muscle in the man's jaw twitched. His smile faltered. But just for a moment.

"Sometimes," he admitted. "I like to wear many hats. It gives me an edge on my competitors. What keeps a client from shopping around more than if you're a one-stop shop?"

Henry couldn't help himself. Try as he might to leave his former life behind, he knew there would always be moments when his old life would bleed through.

"What are you? An infomercial?" he asked with a

snort. "Do I have to give you two payments of $19.99 to get a real answer?"

Just as Michael's cockiness had caused Henry to answer in kind, Henry's new attitude had clearly rubbed the man the wrong way. His smile wiped off. His body tensed.

Henry made sure his grip on the gun was solid.

Not that it would matter.

"What I'm *really* good at isn't information," he said, voice taking on an edge so sharp it felt nearly visible. "It's connections. Creating new ones...and reuniting old ones."

His eyes flitted over Henry's shoulder. By the time he pivoted, gun swinging around with him, it was too late.

Henry froze, his blood turning to ice.

Despite years of training, a lifetime of honing reflexes and learning to listen to his gut, he couldn't move.

"I told him you'd be surprised to see me," the man said in greeting. "It has been a while, hasn't it, partner?"

The ghost of Calvin Fitzgerald smiled.

Though he didn't seem to be as much a ghost as he should have been.

"I know," he continued, taking a step closer. "Confusing, right? Don't worry. I'll explain everything later. For now, I need you out of the way."

Henry wanted to ask a lot of questions.

He didn't mutter a word.

Calvin reached out and patted his shoulder.

"I can't let them kill you, Henry," he chided. Then, like a switch had flipped, the face of Henry's former partner and best friend melted away. In its place was a dark, twisted mask of hatred. "Because *I* want to be the one who does that."

In hindsight, Henry saw the signs that the blow was coming. Saw Calvin make a fist, saw his stance change, and saw the pullback. He saw what was going to happen, seconds before it did. Why? Because he'd seen the man knock out a man before with a perfectly placed hit.

He saw it all.

However, hindsight was only good for the living. It rarely factored in the appearance of ghosts.

## Chapter Seven

Henry remembered the first time he'd met Calvin Fitzgerald. They were both green and, according to their sergeant, had a lot of experience to gain before they could rise through the ranks of their police department. Henry saw it as being told he was beneath par, and *that* hadn't sat well with him. Still, he'd known the pecking order and that only in time would he get higher on it.

*Keep your head down, put in the time, do the work.*

So he'd kept his mouth shut as his then sergeant finished the speech about their lack of experience and dismissed them. As soon as the door shut behind them, Calvin had turned to Henry, grinned and wondered out loud how big the stick was that had taken residence in the sergeant's backside.

It wasn't called for, or professional for that matter, but it lightened the mood enough for normal conversation to take over.

One year later and Henry and Calvin were thick as thieves, best friends, basically brothers.

Then a year after that they were partners. Both heading into the unknown together, each promising to have the other's back no matter what.

One more year passed and then Calvin was dead.

*But he's not.*

It was the first thought that entered the darkness in Henry's mind. The pain waited for him to recall the twisted face of the man who had made a miraculous reappearance in the land of the living before it descended on him. He opened his eyes, wincing but ready.

Though, once again, maybe not.

"Whoa there, deputy," came a woman's rushed whisper. Henry's eyes adjusted to the darkness that hadn't just been in his head. He was leaning against a wall, staring at a strip of stained wallpaper curled and hanging next to his face. He winced again as he moved to get away from it, disoriented. Movement on the other side of the small room started to focus his attention.

Enough light was coming through the broken blinds over the lone window in the room to show him the soft concern across Cassie's face. She crouched down in front of him, one hand reaching out.

"You have a knot on the back of your head," she explained without preamble. Warm fingers touched the spot in question. A sting of pain quickly followed. Her expression softened a little more.

"Calvin," Henry bit out, anger starting to take up the slots he'd let his surprise fall into.

How had he let himself be ambushed like that? How

had he let the man get the upper hand when Henry had been the one armed? How had he let that happen?

"You mean Michael?" Cassie's eyebrow rose.

"Both."

Henry cursed. Cassie shushed him.

"I'm pretty sure they're gone, but still I'd appreciate some inside voices," she told him, stern. That was when Henry saw another emotion he didn't like in the woman.

She was worried.

It deflated his anger.

He needed to get his bearings.

"Are you okay?" he asked. He eyed her stomach before finding her gaze. "What happened? And where are we?"

He sat straighter and reached for his gun.

It was gone.

"I'm freaked out but okay." Cassie stood but kept her voice low. "After you left, I called the department like you said to tell Suzy what was going on. No one answered. The line was dead."

"The line was dead," he repeated, adopting her quiet.

"Not even a busy signal, just dead." A loud rumble sounded at the end of her words. Thunder. It seemed closer this time. Henry got to his feet. "So I called Suzy directly," she continued. "It was busy. That's not unusual, but both Matt Walker's and Deputy Mills' phones are either busy or going straight to voice mail?"

"That *is* unusual," he said.

Cassie nodded, following him to the window. Without pushing the blinds aside he could see a sliver of faded siding on the house next door. They were still in Westbridge.

"That's when I saw Michael drive out of the neighborhood. I got nervous, so I came in after you," she said. "It took me a little bit to find you, but when I did, you were knocked out cold on the grass. So, considering I can't get hold of any backup, I dragged you into the closest house so we weren't just out in the open."

Henry paused, hand in midair in front of the blinds. "Wait, so not only did you *leave* the car, but you knowingly walked into what could have been a trap?" His emotions split in two.

He was angry she'd put herself and the baby in danger.

He couldn't help liking that she had thought he was worth the risk.

Both thoughts immediately turned to a nearly overwhelming feeling of guilt.

He *wasn't* worth it.

Either way, he could see Cassie's indignation at his line of questioning before she even spoke.

"Don't forget I, the pregnant lady, dragged your mass of muscles up a set of back porch stairs, broke into a house and then managed to *gently* lay you down once inside," she shot back, hands going to her hips. "I mean, it wasn't like I could have called you anyways. Not that I'm confident about Carpenter's cell service, but if I remember correctly, you once told me that you *don't have a number.*"

Henry turned back to the blinds, jaw tight.

"We're going to have to talk about that, I promise," he said, voice detaching even to his own ears. "But right now we have bigger fish to fry."

He looked out at the house across from them and the yard between. It was the same one he had walked through. The same one Calvin had used to ambush him. The same Calvin that he'd watched get shot three times in the chest.

Henry shook his head, trying to clear the unnecessary details. It didn't matter *how* Calvin was still alive. What did matter was that he *was* and apparently he didn't want the same for his old partner.

"You said you only saw Michael leave in the car? Are you sure no one else was inside?"

Out of his periphery, a mass of blond curls shook side to side.

"Unless they were lying down in the seats, I didn't see anyone else," she answered. "No one else drove in or out, either. Which is another reason I thought it best for me to get us somewhat hidden. I don't know where Michael's driver went. Like I said, there's no easy way out of the neighborhood other than the entrance, and most of these houses haven't been used in years."

They quieted a moment. Henry was trying to think.

No gun.

He reached into his pocket.

Empty.

No cell phone.

Cassie had one but no one was answering.

Or either couldn't.

Henry's gut grumbled at him. It had already drawn several conclusions. His head injury, no doubt a concussion, was just making it slow to translate them.

"Also, I'd like to point out that *you're* the one who seemingly walked into a trap all willy-nilly, not me."

Henry looked over at Cassie, surprised. She kept her gaze out the window, but she still shrugged.

"All I walked into was a rescue mission, thank you very much."

Despite the situation, Henry smirked.

Their eyes met.

Cassie smiled.

And just like that, they were back in the Eagle, sharing drinks and looks over the pool table. Smiling at each other. Wondering what the rest of the night would bring. Wondering what each other felt like. Tasted like.

Another boom of thunder sounded. This time it felt like it was right outside.

Cassie's smile dropped.

"I also wanted to find you before it started raining," she said. "There are no working lights on this road and with how dark it's getting…" She shook her head. This time her hand went to her stomach, protectively.

Henry pushed his shoulders back again. The pain in

his head pulsed at the movement. No gun, no backup and a storm moving in.

Not great to deal with but also not impossible, either.

"Listen, I want you to call everyone and anyone you know who could send someone out here. Including local PD," he ordered.

Cassie didn't seem to be offended by the direction. She pulled out her phone. "Tell them to come prepared. The man who could still be in here with us is smart, fast and extremely dangerous. His name is Calvin Fitzgerald."

Cassie's eyes widened.

"And be sure to let them know that instead of being dead like we all thought, he is very much alive."

RAIN STARTED TO pelt against the old house's roof. It was like nails on a chalkboard as far as Cassie was concerned. Grating against her nerves that were already starting to fray.

What she had told Henry was the truth. She'd seen Michael leave and couldn't get hold of anyone to alert them to what was going on. When Henry hadn't showed up after that, staying in the car or leaving hadn't been options for Cassie. So she had left her car and snuck around the street and its houses until she'd found the new deputy.

What Cassie *hadn't* told him was that her heart had been in her throat the entire time. That every time she'd turned a corner or rounded a fence, she'd imagined the worst. And that, even when she had finally found him, tears had sprung to her eyes as she'd seen him lying on his back, unmoving, in the grass. That, while she'd hoisted him up and struggled to move him to what she'd thought would be a safe place for both of them, she'd done so with a worry and fear in her heart unlike she'd ever felt before.

The entire world had fallen away in that time, leaving only three people who mattered. Her unborn son, her body that cradled him and Henry.

Now, after another one of her friends' phones went to voice mail and the rain continued to beat down overhead, the rest of the world was starting to filter back in.

And with it an uncertainty that made her want to cling to her belly and the man who had given her the very son she wanted to keep safe inside it.

"There's no movement from the houses on either side of us or across the street. If Calvin is around here, he's keeping low."

Cassie turned, startled, as the man from her thoughts walked back into what had once been a living room. His face was pinched. His brow lined with worry.

She wasn't about to help those lines, either.

"Unless everyone decided to turn off their phones or make lengthy calls, I think something is wrong with Carpenter's service," she said. "Or at least the department's. I can't even get the local PD to pick up. Which makes no sense."

The lines of worry deepened.

"Has anything like this happened before?"

Cassie shrugged. "Yes and no. While I was a trainee, we got a rough batch of tornadoes that caused an almost county-wide blackout. Landlines went down and a lot of people lost cell service." She motioned to the window and outside. "But this storm just came up on us. It couldn't have already done that kind of damage. Heck, I doubt even now it could." She let out a frustrated sigh. "So what *is* going on out there?"

Henry's expression went blank. His body subtly shifted to more alert. "I don't know, but staying here isn't helping us. I'm going to go get the car." He raised his hand to silence her before Cassie could open her mouth. "And this time you are staying put."

"You do remember how that turned out last time, right? You said it yourself that we don't know where Calvin is. He could be simply waiting for you to show up again."

Henry kept his hand up, unperturbed. "Last time was different." His voice took on a hard edge. Angry. But she couldn't tell at who or what. "Now I know who we're playing with. I won't let Calvin get the better of me. Not again."

He dropped his hand and knelt to the bottom of his pant leg. He pulled it up, showing off a knife holstered to his ankle.

"Calvin hates knives," he explained, unfastening it. "He was jumped by a perp with one when we were beat cops. Got messed up pretty badly. Ever since then he won't touch them. Won't hold them."

"So he didn't take it off you," she finished.

"A lot apparently has happened in the last year to him, but that fear seems to have held true."

He stood and handed her the knife. Cassie didn't like them, either, but she disliked being defenseless more. She took it, but before she could pull away, he held on to her hand, his fingers against her skin. Their warmth spread from his touch across her body like a wildfire.

Cassie suddenly remembered what it was like to have those same fingers move across her body.

Nimble.

Strong.

Intoxicating.

"Don't come after me this time." Henry's voice thrummed, a soothing baritone. If he was struggling with memories, it didn't show. His expression stayed blank. "I mean it, Cassie."

She didn't want to agree, but then his eyes turned down to her stomach for the briefest of moments.

This time Cassie knew she would listen.

Henry must have seen the decision in her face. He let his hand drop.

"I'll come inside and get you," he said, already moving away.

Cassie wanted to stop him. Wanted to talk. To tell him how hurt she'd been when he'd never called or tried to contact her. To tell him that, even though he obviously hadn't wanted to be with her, now they would always be connected by their son.

But it wasn't the right time.

Would it ever be?

Did she ever *want* it to be?

She watched as the father of her child ran out the back door and disappeared into the rain. Now was the time to focus on danger, not feelings.

So Cassie gripped the handle of the knife and waited.

## Chapter Eight

The rain washed the lasagna off most of Henry's pants. It was the only silver lining he could come up with as he drove into Westbridge and into the driveway of the house Cassie was in. If Calvin was around, he'd decided not to make his presence known. Or maybe he'd realized the rain, growing heavier by the minute, could just as easily be an advantage or a disadvantage.

One night, as partners, Henry and Calvin had discussed using weather as a cover for a raid. Calvin was for it, yet Henry hadn't liked the idea. Sure, rain caused low visibility, which meant the target couldn't be 100 percent alert. But, by the same token, that meant the one executing the plan couldn't be, either. Same with trying to get the drop on someone at night.

It was hard to keep your bearings if you never had them all the way down in the first place.

When you were dealing with armed, well-trained people, it was best to have as much control over the situation as you could. A stance that Henry and

Calvin had disagreed on right up until the day that changed everything.

Henry's grip tightened around the steering wheel.

He didn't like the rain now.

Just as he didn't like the idea that Calvin could be lurking within it.

Cassie had the front door open before Henry was done jogging up. He was glad to see the knife in her hand still, but that she was also calm.

"No one made a peep," she confirmed, voice rising above the rain as they ran to the car together.

She went straight to the back seat on the driver's side. Henry took lead and slid behind the wheel.

"I don't like this," she added after he hit Reverse and then straightened on the street. "Did they say anything to you before Calvin attacked you?" Her voice softened. Honey. "And didn't you say that Calvin was your partner? What's he doing here? And alive?"

"I can only answer about half of that," Henry hated to admit.

"Then I'll take those answers."

Henry turned out of the neighborhood and directed them back toward the department. The sky behind them was almost black, but in the distance it looked like the clouds were wanting to part. Leave it to the temperamental Southern weather to keep everyone on their toes.

"The man named Michael said he was a broker, one who made connections," he started, keeping his eyes on the street ahead. The last thing they needed was to get into an accident while out of communications and drenched. "That's when Calvin showed up. Yes, we used to be partners, but then he was killed in the line of duty. Or so I thought. His body was never recovered, but—" Henry stopped and tried to find the right words to explain what had happened next. It was a hard task. "But with everything going on, there was a good chance the fire took care of it."

"The fire," Cassie repeated, hesitation in her tone. Still, she didn't form it into a question.

"He'd been shot in the chest three times and wasn't wearing a vest," he continued. "So when we couldn't find his body and he didn't show up…" Henry slammed his hand against the wheel. "I stopped looking for his body one measly month after everything happened. I should have kept on. If I had known there was a chance he was still out there…"

"It sounds like you had very valid reasons for assuming he wasn't. Anyone in your shoes probably would have done the same. Beating yourself up about it won't help us figure out what's going on *now.*" Again her voice went to honey. Soothing and sweet. "Did he talk to you before you lost consciousness?"

Henry ignored the shame from the question but nodded. His jaw set. "He doesn't want them, whoever they are, to kill me—" he pushed the words through his clenched teeth "—because he wants to be the one who kills me."

Silence filled the small car. Henry kept his eyes forward, navigating back into traffic. The rain lessened. Sunlight could be seen breaking through the clouds in the distance.

It wasn't until they were going down the street in front of the sheriff's department that Cassie spoke again. There was no hint of honey in her words.

"I'm worried about my friends and the department right now and why neither seems to be picking up their phones," she said. "So we're going to make sure everything is okay. But, Henry? After that we're going to have a talk."

There was no room to interpret it as a request.

So he didn't. "Yes, ma'am."

EVERYTHING WASN'T ALL RIGHT.

There was a group of deputies standing at the back of the parking lot. Through the rain and distance Cassie could tell some were angry by the sets of their stances or the scowls on their faces. But that didn't mean she was about to go over to see what for. Cassie didn't want to stay in the rain to find out when she was on her own timeline, being possibly one of the only two people who knew there was a not-deceased Calvin and mystery man Michael in Riker County. With bad intentions to boot.

Henry seemed to be on the same wavelength as far as getting inside was concerned. After parking in the first open spot in the guest lot, he kept so close to Cassie that she ran into him twice on her way to the front door. His closeness would normally set off memories of their shared night together, if the last day was any indication, but Cassie found comfort in it now.

The lobby wasn't lacking in activity, either. Henry took lead and guided Cassie past deputies, civilians and a man she recognized as a reporter from the TV station next door. He didn't stop until they were in the hallway that ran past the main offices. Frustration could be heard clear as a bell through Suzy's open door. Cassie went straight for it.

"—can tell Dean Carver that if he wants to let everyone know it was intentional and start a panic, then by all means go ahead and make our jobs harder!"

Suzy slammed her open hand across the desktop while Captain Dane Jones nodded to the sentiment. They both looked like they had aged years since Cassie and Henry had left that morning.

Henry cleared his throat.

Suzy's demeanor changed so swiftly that the man hesitated in his opening.

"Where have you two been?" Suzy asked, eyes scanning them with open concern. It probably didn't help matters that both were soaked to the bone. "Mills said he saw you peel off in your car."

Cassie hoped she hid her embarrassment at what, in hindsight, hadn't been the smartest idea. Still, she wasn't going to lie. "The man that gave me the ring—Michael—was in the parking lot. Deputy Ward tried to talk to him, but he ran off." She tried an indifferent shrug. "So I pursued them both."

Suzy opened her mouth but Henry butted in before she could get a word out.

"He had a driver and we followed them back to the neighborhood of Westbridge," he hurriedly related. "I went in after them and was knocked out."

"But not before he identified the second man as Calvin Fitzgerald," Cassie added.

Dane raised his eyebrow.

"Calvin as in—" he started.

"That Calvin," Henry finished.

Cassie didn't feel like recapping this same conversation, so she moved to the part she didn't understand.

"We tried to call it in, but the phones aren't working here?" she asked. "And everyone else's were off or busy."

Suzy flipped back to angry.

"The fiber optic cables that run to the building were severed," Dane said with a good dose of the same anger. "It took out our internet and phones."

"Since then our personal phones have been tied up by each other and the public," Suzy added. "It took me twenty minutes just to get a call out to James and the kids."

"Wait, fiber optic cables are buried in the ground," Henry pointed out. "They just don't get severed on accident."

Suzy and Dane both tensed, the latter's hand fisted.

"Unless someone *accidentally* brought in an excavator to the back of the building and cut them, I'd say it was intentional," Dane said.

A moment of thought stretched between all of them. First Billy, then Calvin and Michael, and now this? What was going on in Riker County?

THE RAIN MIGHT have pelted the houses in Westbridge, and even fallen at a good enough clip to hide the ruckus and the sight of an excavator digging at the department, but not even one drop had fallen at Cassie's house. Her hanging plants, on either side of the front door, were drooping something awful.

"One thing you can count on about the weather in Alabama during July is that you can't count on the weather in Alabama during July," Cassie told herself as she parked her car in the driveway and sighed.

The day had not gone the way it should have, not at all. Instead of her bringing some much-needed cheer to her colleagues and friends that morning, the department was now trying to keep its head above water without communications, ghosts apparently were walking free through the town with evil intent and her front seat was covered in lasagna.

She rubbed her belly.

And she was still hungry.

Movement outside the car finally coaxed Cassie to get out. Another item to add to the list of things that had taken an unexpected turn was the continued appearance of Deputy Henry Ward. She watched as he looked at her house. One-story, boxy and painted a calming light blue, it was small but had gotten the job done for the last five years. Then again, she'd lived alone during those years. Add in a baby and the home she loved dearly might become the home she wished had another bedroom.

"This is one of the newer neighborhoods in Carpenter," she found herself explaining, sidling up to the man. Their clothes had had enough time to dry to the point they weren't dripping everywhere like faucets. Still, Cassie would bet his personal car parked at the curb was just as wet as hers. "It was built to be its own miniature community with a fancy pool and clubhouse in the middle, kind of like what Florida does with theirs, but the developer's funding still hasn't gone all the way through yet." She motioned down the street. Her house was one of six in the area, beyond which were empty lots with For Sale signs staking out each plot. "You're looking at the crazy few who took a chance. Though I think maybe we just all really wanted a pool."

Henry smiled but didn't laugh. His thoughts weren't hanging around the small, undeveloped neighborhood, she knew. Still, it bothered her.

"Do you live in Carpenter?" she ventured. "Or do you commute from one of the other towns?"

"I'm staying in a hotel until I can find something," he answered.

It sounded rehearsed. She guessed he'd been asked several times already.

"Can't beat the location and it's way better than what

I was used to back in Tennessee. That's one good thing about undercover, it makes you appreciate the simple joys of a somewhat normal life." Henry's demeanor changed in tandem with Cassie's eyebrows rising clear to her hairline.

Did he just say he'd been undercover?

"But you know, again the hotel is only temporary," he hurried to tack on. "It even has some good food, so I can't complain. So, does your sister live here with you? Didn't you say she lived in Carpenter?"

It was an attempted switch of topics. One Cassie wouldn't have stood for normally. However, being reminded of Kristen was enough to get her on board with the change.

"She doesn't live with me, but she *does* live close." Cassie pointed to the house across the street. "And she works from home mostly, so I suggest we hurry inside before she walks past her windows and sees us. Plus, I'd be lying if I didn't say if I don't eat something soon, things are going to turn dangerous for you and anyone else around me."

Cassie thought her bit of humor would do the trick, lightening the deputy's mood enough that whatever walls he had up around him would drop. Or, at least, create a doorway for her to go through. But no sooner had they gotten inside her front door than it was like someone had set his feet in concrete.

His jaw was set. Hard.

Like he'd just realized he'd made a mistake.

Cassie couldn't deny it stung.

"I can't stay," he said, resolute. "I need to help with the department, but I just wanted to make sure you got here okay… And I promised you we'd talk. I'd like to keep that promise."

Every question Cassie had for the man flew through her head in quick succession. She *knew* what she wanted to ask, yet, as she stared up into eyes that cooled the Alabama heat that had followed them inside, all she wanted in that moment was to be in his arms. To touch him. To kiss him. To know what she had felt all those months ago was real.

Yet he didn't give her the chance to utter a word.

"I can't do it right now. But before I can leave this house, I have to ask—" Henry broke his invisible mold long enough to take a step closer.

Cassie's thoughts scattered, leaving her utterly unprepared for the one question she should have seen coming.

Henry squared his shoulders and, with a look that was nothing but vulnerable, he finally asked it. "Cassie, am I the father?"

So, standing in her entryway with what felt like a town-size number of questions just outside her door, Cassie decided it was time for them to have at least one answer. Even if she had to give it herself.

"Yes."

## *Chapter Nine*

One word.

That was all it took.

One word turned Henry's mind from worries about the surprise that was Calvin, from worries about the two men who were still at large for crippling communications at the department, and even from thinking certain charged thoughts about the woman standing in front of him.

The woman carrying his child.

A son.

Henry liked to think he was an honorable man. One who would say the right thing, do the right thing. Or at least who had the workings where he could eventually be that person. When he was younger he thought he knew what he wanted in the future. To be a cop, to fight for the people who couldn't, to meet a great woman, settle down and have a family.

Since then none of that had changed. Instead the only thing that had shifted was his belief that he deserved any of it. Henry had spent the last several years in between long stints of working as an undercover cop.

He'd toed the line between right and wrong, all in the name of trying to get justice. He'd seen bad and he'd seen worse. He'd done some of his own to keep his cover intact, turning his back on the lesser crimes to help build a case against the bigger ones. Calvin had been there, too, making the same day-by-day choices, weighing the good against the bad. The bad versus the greater good.

Sometimes it had torn Henry up to pretend he was just like the people and groups he'd had to infiltrate. Mean men and women. Greedy and selfish. Angry.

Sometimes he'd felt like he was losing himself, drowning in grown-up make-believe where every action had a potentially dangerous consequence.

Other times it had been easy.

He'd been able to play the role of "bad guy" even better than some of those he was trying to take down.

Too easy.

It was because of those times that Henry now felt shame burning in his chest. He didn't have to have known Cassie for years, like her friends did, to know she was one of the good ones. She knew where the lines were and stayed on the right side of them.

Soft skin, pink lips and green, green eyes that probably tried to see the best in everyone.

Cassie Gates was too good for him.

So how could he be good for their child?

The internal war of thoughts Henry's mind exploded with only took seconds. If he was being honest with himself, he had already known the moment he'd seen her protruding belly. Getting confirmation from her had only given him permission to finally listen to what he'd already thought about the night before.

Still, he let the silence almost suffocate them until Cassie had had enough. Her expression pinched, her nostrils flared and the very lips he couldn't get out of his mind thinned.

"I would have told you, but as it turns out, I don't know you." With one graceful movement she reached around him and opened the front door again.

Henry should have said something—anything—but the words never came. He took Cassie's lead and left, chest filled with regret this time.

TRAVIS NEWMAN WAS caught trying to shimmy down a drainpipe off an office building like some kind of trained monkey. All Deputy Maria Medina had had to do was reach out and grab the man's pants before slinging him to the ground. There he'd put up a fight, but it had only been a halfhearted one. It was hard to tussle with your pants ripped right across the backside.

The excavator Travis had stolen and then used at the sheriff's department had been linked to a construction company in the town of Darby, just beyond the town limits. The office manager had been able to get footage of the nighttime robbery off a well-hidden security camera. It had been the lone one not destroyed by Travis's accomplice, a woman wearing a ski mask and boots. She had stood on the outskirts of the property while Travis did the heavy lifting, so to speak.

From there tracking down Travis had been easy enough. He was what the sheriff's department called a frequent flier. They knew his face, his name and where he lived. Not including or limited to his predilection for prescription pills, public intoxication and domestic violence when it came to his on-again, off-again girlfriend, Sara.

"And now suddenly he wants to take an excavator to the back of the sheriff's department?" Henry shook his head. "Doesn't seem to fit with what you all have told me about the man."

Henry was leaning on the edge of his desk in the bull pen, one of three deputies making up a half circle around him. Caleb Foster was the most severe of them. Henry had no doubt he knew things weren't adding up. He turned to his partner, Dante Mills, with a frown. "I know I haven't been here as long as you, but am I wrong to say that I didn't think Travis even knew what fiber optics were? Let alone where to dig to get to them and cut them?"

Dante shook his head.

"That's some out-of-the-box thinking for a Newman," he confirmed. "His lady might know a thing or two more."

Caleb's eyebrow rose at that. "Last I heard, Sara left

Travis high and dry for that McGinty kid over in Bates Hill. You know, the one who got naked and ran through the parade last year."

Dante shook his head again. "My grandma said Rebecca, over at the salon, heard that her sister talked to someone who saw Sara necking with one of the Marlow brothers at the drive-in in Darby."

"Oh, you mean the ones who opened that new hardware store in Kipsy?"

Dante gave him a thumbs-up. "That's them."

Caleb looked impressed.

"Good for Sara," he said approvingly. "I heard both brothers are good guys. Alyssa had to meet them for work and said they were really respectful and seemed to know their stuff."

Henry watched their back and forth like a tennis match. Other than Alyssa, Caleb's wife, he didn't recognize the other names. That wasn't unusual for a community like Riker County. Small towns, tight-knit communities and gossip that stayed as strong and steady as a river's current. One day he'd be able to get into the lingo with the best of them, but for now it made him feel very much like the new guy he was. The useless, beneath-par new guy who had already broken protocol that morning, getting the pregnant dispatcher to chase danger.

Though Henry doubted he could have stopped Cassie from doing just what she had done.

Then again, he should have at least tried.

Henry cleared his throat and pushed off his desk.

"So, guessing that Travis was given orders to follow isn't a far-fetched notion," he offered. Both men shook their heads.

"He has a sister, but she lives out of state. Tennessee, I think," Caleb said. His attention caught on Captain Jones across the room. While the sheriff was openly charismatic and personable, the captain was openly gruff and introspective. He carried a box now, head bent and eyes not caring to take in the bustle of deputies and personnel around him. His mind was clearly on something else. Caleb seemed to be interested in that unknown topic. He was already turning his body away as he finished his thought. "Matt is tracking her down, though. I think Maggie is helping from home, too, since our internet and phones are on the fritz. Hey, Jones!"

Caleb took off, Dante on his heels. Henry surveyed the bull pen, but his thoughts went straight out of the building and to a small box house on a street with five other small box houses.

Cassie Gates. Soft skin, lips that tasted as good as they felt, and hair that he'd been happily tangled in. A woman who had wielded humor, compassion and a quick wit with ease the night they had met.

A woman who had taken a grieving man and given him hope that he could still find some happiness.

If only he deserved it.

Henry shook his head, growing angry at himself. Not only did he think he didn't deserve the touch of a woman as pure as Cassie, but he didn't need to even think about that touch. Not right now. Not when the department he had pledged himself to was going to hell in a handbasket.

He needed to focus. Distractions had already cost him his best friend and partner. Though, after running into that same best friend and partner, Henry wondered what else he had missed about the man while they were undercover.

Thunder grumbled above the building. The sound of heavy equipment and ground crews outside trying to restore what Travis had destroyed didn't waver. All calls from the sheriff's department jurisdiction had been temporarily rerouted to the local police departments in each town while deputies on patrol kept their cell phones close at hand. Still, even the workers outside knew the precarious situation they were in.

Having no communications was one thing.

Having your trusted law enforcement have no communications was another.

"Hey, Ward."

Detective Walker stood in the open door of his office and waved him over. He was shaking his head already.

"Detective Ansler just finished his sweep of Westbridge with a few other deputies," Matt told him as he neared. "The only person they found was a female squatter we're familiar with. She said she didn't see anything or even know you and Cassie were there earlier. I'm inclined to believe her, since we've never had an issue with her honesty before. *But* Ansler is bringing her in anyways. She might know something she doesn't even know." Matt shifted his attention to the cell phone in his hand. "Suzy should be bringing our friend Travis back to the interrogation room for round two right about now. I couldn't be present for the first time, but for this one I want to see his reaction when Suzy asks him about Calvin."

"She hasn't asked if there's a connection there yet?" Henry was surprised at that.

"No. Suzy has her own system when it comes to getting answers, though." Matt clapped him on the shoulder reassuringly. "She's a grade-A button pusher. I'm pretty sure she learned half of her interrogation skills from her nine-year-old." He smiled at a memory Henry wasn't privy to, but then sobered. "Why don't you come along and watch with me? I'd like to have you in there when she throws out Calvin's name. Him showing up at the same time a no-brain like Travis attacks the department is a coincidence I don't like or accept. If there's a connection, I want to make sure we're looking at it from every possible angle."

"Yeah, I'd like to come," Henry agreed. "Thanks."

Matt gave him a smile as they moved back through the bull pen. It was brief but true enough. "I don't know how you're used to working in your undercover stints, but here we rarely go lone wolf to get a job done."

A laugh bubbled up behind them.

"Yeah, none of us has ever gone lone wolf in this

department," Suzanne Simmons deadpanned. A look passed between the chief deputy and Matt as she fell into step at their side. "I can't even recall any one instance where one of us decided to figure out things by ourselves."

Matt put his hands up, obviously guilty.

"Okay, so *sometimes* a few of us have decided to err on the side of keeping information close to our chest until we get better bearings," he admitted. He pointed at Henry, mock sternness pulling his brow tight. He shook his finger like a teacher would when instructing a student. "But when things got too hairy, we always knew to call in the cavalry. Standing alone in the face of danger when you have a building full of people to back you up isn't always the smartest decision."

Henry couldn't help grinning. "That sounded like something you would read in a fortune cookie."

Suzy snorted. Matt shrugged.

"Doesn't make it any less true," Matt said.

The moment they walked into the hallway that led to the interrogation room, the humor dissipated. Like they'd shucked invisible coats and were about to be forced to enter the cold.

"Travis's lawyer should be here by the end of the hour," Suzy said, voice lowering the closer they got. "Pay attention to everything and anything. He's not the smartest guy in the county, but after what he pulled, maybe we haven't been giving him enough credit the last few years."

Henry had started to agree when voices and footsteps pulled their attention to the end of the hallway. Deputy Medina rounded the corner, directing a man who must have been Travis at her side. She nodded to them, totally unaware of the change in her perp's expression.

A shock of adrenaline charged Henry's system as the man met his eyes.

"Gage?" the man called Travis rasped.

No hint of suspicion, betrayal or anger colored the twenty-something's face. All Henry could read was surprise. Sincere surprise.

It was because of this surprise that several things happened at once.

First and foremost, Henry's thoughts went to his clothes. He was wearing a pair of jeans his brother had often said made him look like some kind of cowboy doing a Levi's ad. Women in the past had more or less given him the same comment, though their attention to the details had been less analytical and more on the sensual side. Henry wasn't above trying to entice the opposite sex using a pair of jeans, but that wasn't why he loved them. They fit well, were the color of worn denim, and always made a pair of boots look good.

He'd had them for years but hadn't thought to break them out at his new job. That had been Cassie's fault. Or, at least, her lasagna. Once he'd gotten back to the department, he'd changed out of his soiled uniform and into his plain clothes. Since there were more important issues being addressed, no one had ordered him to change.

Which was good, considering that what he was about to try to do required him to *not* be in uniform.

The second and third things that happened next did so in quick succession. Henry stopped in his tracks so suddenly that Matt bumped into his elbow. Suzy, a step behind, stepped on the back of his boot.

There was no time to explain himself.

He just hoped he wasn't about to get fired.

Or worse, shot.

Riding the wave of confusion, Henry turned on his heel and fisted his hand.

Matt never saw the punch coming.

## Chapter Ten

"What?"

Kristen Gates's mouth hung open like she was trying to catch something. A few seconds before, a noise escaped the open trap that Cassie couldn't easily define. It wasn't exactly a shriek but not a yell, either.

Maybe screech was a more applicable descriptor.

Either way it made Cassie fight the urge to cover her ears.

Maybe telling someone about her day hadn't been the best idea.

Or, maybe, it was her choosing her older sister to tell that hadn't been the right call. Kristen was already dramatic in her own right. Never mind adding *actual* drama to the mix.

"I'm fine," Cassie reassured Kristen again. They were sitting in her living room, untouched sweet and decaf tea beside them. The rain had stayed away from their houses, but Cassie had a feeling nothing now would have stopped Kristen from crossing the street to get to her. It was like she had a sixth sense for excitement. Even if it hadn't happened to her.

Cassie made a sweeping gesture to include her stomach. "Again, we're fine," she said.

Kristen, a woman made up of long limbs, wild blond hair and a nose that had earned her the nickname of Mrs. Beaks in middle school, was notably trying to hold in the rushing waters of sibling protectiveness. She opened her mouth, closed it, opened it again and started to turn red.

Cassie mused that the older woman looked like she was sucking on a lemon while simultaneously trying to scold an errant child.

She didn't know if she should be afraid or flattered. Or both.

However, she felt neither reaction.

If Cassie hadn't been emotionally gutted hours before by the brooding Deputy Ward and his utter lack of response when learning he was the father of her child, she might have been amused by her sister's overreaction. As it was, she sank even farther back into the plushness of her living room chair and waited out the storm.

"What makes you think that going after those men was all right?" Kristen finally said, landing on anger again. "They could have had guns! They could have shot at you! And chasing them in your crappy little Honda, too! That in itself is bad enough. Did you forget about that one time *when it caught fire*? And that was when it was going through Mom and Dad's neighborhood! Where it's like ten miles an hour! It's a miracle it didn't combust pushing eighty!"

Kristen's face reddened into a dangerous shade of crimson. Her chest began to heave. She had officially entered into angry-worried, an emotional state that Cassie was used to being on the receiving end of thanks to being the baby of the family. Her brothers entered that state every time she'd dated a boy they didn't like or been caught sneaking off to a party. Who needed parents when your big brothers were always ready to give you a stern talking to?

For once, though, angry-worried wasn't unwarranted.

Yet the part of Cassie that resented being babied, especially by someone only a year older than she, reared its head long enough to defend herself.

"It was *one* time and it didn't catch fire! It overheated and puffed out smoke. That was it."

"I saw flames!"

Cassie opened her mouth to attempt another defensive strike even if it was a halfhearted attempt. Once Kristen Gates had something to talk about, especially when it came to venting, she wouldn't stop until everything was out on the table.

But the older woman didn't give her the chance at a rebuttal.

"That's not the point, Cassie. Flames or not, you shouldn't have followed. You should have let that man go it alone."

Cassie had a moment of déjà vu. The fear and anguish at finding Henry unconscious in Westbridge hitting her like a ton of bricks again. If she hadn't been there? What would have happened?

Then again, if she had never showed up at the side of the street and driven them to that very same neighborhood?

Guilt extended the worry behind each *what-if*.

One or all of the emotions must have showed in her expression. Kristen took a beat, visibly restraining herself. She inhaled a long breath and sat on the edge of the coffee table. When she let the breath out, her face lost some of its redness.

"Cassie," she started again. Their knees touched. It was the grounding Kristen must have needed. When she spoke, her words softened. "You have always been the sweetest, most compassionate out of the Gates kids. Something you no doubt learned from Dad. I mean, we don't just call you Daddy's girl for kicks. Your desire to see the best in everyone and even encourage it is a trait you and Dad have become pros at. You two put all of us above yourself.

"I mean, even when we were kids you always made sure we were happy before even thinking about you. What normal eighteen-year-old skips her own prom to throw her, at times admittedly ungrateful, older sister a surprise birthday party? Or who turns down a once-in-a-lifetime date with the hot, sexy fireman Marcus

Guiles to drive over a hundred miles because you knew Davie didn't have anyone to help him move?"

She grinned. "At the best of times your heart and capacity to empathize and help the people around you have kept you from getting something you want." Kristen reached out and purposely touched the scar at Cassie's neck. "At the worst of times it has nearly cost you your life." She dropped her hand.

Cassie took the moment to touch the same scar.

"That was different, and you know it," she reminded Kristen. "I was trying to protect Billy's little girl."

Once again Kristen's expression softened.

"I know," she said. "But what about today?"

They both lapsed into silence.

Cassie didn't want to break it. She didn't want to admit why she had done what she had. Why she had wanted to help Henry.

Kristen took the silence as contemplation. She continued when it was clear Cassie wouldn't. "You can't help everyone, Cassie. Especially not strangers with troubled pasts." She smiled. It was a warm look. "There're two of you now. That's double the danger in everything you do."

Cassie let out a sigh of defeat.

The willpower she had long held on to since she'd found out she was pregnant had just cracked. While she hadn't kept her pregnancy a secret from her family and friends, she had censored the part about the one-night stand with a stranger. Instead she had said the father was a friend and one who didn't want a family. A decision they both had decided was best. No hard feelings.

It hadn't mattered, of course. Cassie's brothers, and most of her sheriff's department colleagues and friends, had roared. Threats and promises of pain had swiftly followed. Even her parents, even a parent as kindly as her dad, had had very bad words for the mystery man she refused to name.

But now that Cassie had found Henry?

Now that he lived in the same zip code?

Now that he worked in the same building?

Now everything was different.

"His name is Henry and he's not a stranger, Kristen. At least, not in the ways that count." Cassie let her gaze drop to her stomach.

Kristen's eyes soon followed. They widened when she understood. "Oh."

Cassie rubbed her stomach. "Oh is right."

A moment passed. Then Kristen stood, grabbed her glass of sweet tea and started to retreat into the kitchen.

"What are you doing?" Cassie asked, worried she'd somehow broken her sister.

"I'm exchanging this for two glasses of wine," she called over her shoulder before disappearing into the next room. "I feel like you need a drink."

"Kristen, I'm seven months' pregnant!"

Kristen's mass of hair floated into view as she popped her head around the corner. "I know! I'm drinking for both of us!"

HIS JAW WAS THROBBING. There would be a bruise across his skin. If there wasn't already one. If he could have, he would have touched the tender spot. Instead he slid his jaw back and forth with a grunt.

He also tasted a little blood.

Suzanne Simmons had one hell of a right cross.

"You know, they ain't supposed to be able to do that," Travis said.

Henry looked across the interrogation table. Travis eyed the spot where Suzy had hauled off and hit Henry in retaliation for punching her lead detective. It had happened so fast that Henry genuinely didn't have time to dodge it, for show or not.

The surprise and pain had coupled to make him stagger. He'd barely regained his footing when the newly recovered Matt had jumped in to subdue him. But not without a fight from Henry. He'd bucked against the detective all the way into the interrogation room and didn't stop until his hands were cuffed behind the chair.

Even then Henry had used his words to fight. Calling Matt and Suzy a lot of not-so-great things.

By then he'd hoped they'd understood what he was doing.

If not, he was definitely fired.

Or really under arrest.

"They can't just touch you like that and then lock you away," Travis restated. His eyes shifted to the mirror behind Henry. Suzy, Matt and Deputy Medina were all watching, he was sure. "That's what they did to

Ricky, 'member? Jumped him and got all crazy when he fought back." He shook his head, disgusted. "Self-defense! That's all it was! How is that right that they locked *him* up and threw away the key? Tell me that!" Travis shook his head, hair slapping the sides of his head. It was shorter than it had been the last time Henry had seen him.

"These pigs think they can do whatever they want," Henry agreed, slipping into a heavier Southern twang. "Think they're above the law."

Travis ate it up. His head switched movements. He nodded so hard it made his cuffs *clink* against his chair.

"It's supposed to be innocent until proven guilty," he railed. "Just wait. My lawyer will get here and sort it out." The questions Travis should have had at seeing someone from his past finally seemed to dawn across his expression. His thin face almost caved in on itself, pinching in confusion. "Wait, what did you do? Why're you here?" He lowered his voice to a quick whisper, eyeing the glass behind Henry. "Last I heard, you'd got a new job."

For a split second Henry worried that Travis had figured it out, that he was a deputy, not the small-time drug runner Gage Coulson. But if there was one thing he was certain about, it was that Travis wasn't smart enough to hide what he did and did not know.

He *knew* Henry as a man he'd worked with for a year.

He *didn't know* that Gage wasn't real. Just a persona and an identity that had been created as a part of a task force to stop a dangerous organization from getting traction in Tennessee.

What *Henry knew* was that Suzy had been wrong. Not only was Travis not smart enough to bluff; he wasn't clever or organized enough to cripple the sheriff's department's communications. Not by himself.

He was more of a paint-by-numbers kind of guy.

And even then Henry had seen him mess that up from time to time.

Still, he needed to be a little cautious. Considering the last time he'd seen the man was right before the ambush.

"You heard what went down at the warehouse?" he asked, searching the man's expression for any tells. "After the fire?"

Travis nodded then shrugged.

"Everybody heard about that," he said. Again he eyed the two-way mirror. He'd been arrested enough to know that people were watching. Still, he wasn't smart enough to know that whispering wouldn't keep the people on the other side from hearing them. Or that maybe he should just keep his mouth shut altogether. "They said it was a trap, got swarmed by cops after I took off. Grabbed a group of y'all. Even nabbed some of those Richland fellas." He spit off to the side, a curse to the Richlands. "Ain't gonna lie, I was okay with that." He managed to drop an almost apologetic look. "Was sorry to hear about Parker, though. No way to go, I suspect. Burning alive like that. Heard they never found his body."

Henry didn't have to pretend that the memory pained him. To keep their partnership intact during their time undercover, Henry and Calvin had been named as brothers. Gage and Parker Coulson had become friends and business associates with the very people they were trying to take down. Calvin had been better at being friendly. Maybe *that* was how he'd escaped.

Because he surely hadn't used Travis's help.

The man seemed genuine in his belief that Henry *wasn't* a cop and that Calvin had died that day.

Which meant Calvin hadn't included the small-time crook in his plan. At least, if he had, not directly.

"They said the fire did the job," Henry said, careful in his words. "No remains left but ash."

Travis shook his head in sympathy. Curiosity soon replaced it. "What happened to you? Heard you was let go and left town."

"Yeah, those cops couldn't find nothing on me." Henry scrunched his nose like he smelled something disgusting. "They tried, though, but you know how smart Parker was. Dead or alive, he wasn't about to let his little brother get locked up." Henry lowered his voice to the point where he questioned whether Suzy and the rest of their audience *could* hear him on the other side of the mirror. "I had enough alibis to squeeze out of town. The Richlands, not so much."

Travis let out a hoot of laughter. His handcuffs *clinked* against the metal of his chair again.

"So I came to 'Bama, thinking the change in scenery would be good," Henry continued. "Then there I am, just checking out the situation with the local black-and-whites, when *bam!* I get grabbed again. Something about being a suspect. Calling me a thief and conspirator." Henry mispronounced the last word, adding enough Southern twang to make it seem like he was barely capable enough to know what it meant, let alone be it. His goal of getting down to why Travis had attacked the department would only be met if he stayed true to the most important principle of what had made him a successful Gage Coulson.

Travis had to be able to relate to him. Get on the same page. Henry had to show the man that even though time had passed and their situation had changed, Henry was still of the same mind.

The same side, too.

"Said someone took out their phones here," he added, sure to put some awe in his tone. "Now they're all running around like chickens with their heads cut off."

Travis couldn't help himself. He grinned.

Not only was it important to be able to relate to a dense criminal, it was also important to inflate their ego sometimes, too. Henry couldn't resist the latter.

"Told them it wasn't me, but I'll tell you what, that must have taken a lot of brains to pull that off." Henry gave him a wink. "Got them scrambling around like crazy. Believe you me, that's someone I wouldn't mind working for."

Pride, clear as day, pushed Travis's chest out.

Then something unexpected happened.

That pride was replaced with worry, followed swiftly by fear. It creased his brow and sagged his body down.

"You always been nice to me, Gage. So I'll keep it fair between us." Travis leaned over as far as he could.

Henry mirrored him, another surge of adrenaline starting to swirl inside his chest. When the man spoke again, his words were so low Henry almost had a hard time following.

"Might be time to leave town again. The people running this thing got a big plan for everyone here. As soon as it gets dark, all hell will be raining down. You don't wanna be around when that happens."

It wasn't a threat.

It was a promise.

## Chapter Eleven

"He's not that dumb."

Henry dropped into one of the several seats around the conference room table. Luckily, he was neither in cuffs nor being fired. At least, not yet.

"Even Travis knows he pushed the limits with what he should and shouldn't have said," Henry continued. "With how quick he buttoned his trap closed just now, I think he's done talking."

Suzy kept standing next to the head of the table. Matt, Caleb, Dante and Deputy Medina took the open seats around him.

"I think you're right," the chief deputy agreed. "I don't think I'm going out on a limb here when I point out that man was afraid. Whether that fear is for the people he's answering to or for the supposed rest of the plan, or both, I'm not sure. But yeah, I think he's done."

"Even if he wasn't, his lawyer will make him shut up," Medina added. "We got lucky enough that he was caught in traffic and it added a few minutes to his commute. We definitely couldn't have pulled off that little show otherwise."

Henry agreed with that. After Travis had shut down, his lawyer showed up. Deputy Medina had explained why Henry had been thrown into the room with Travis by blaming the chaos of everyone running around, trying to do their jobs without their normal tools. It was vague and really didn't make that much sense, but Maria had sold it with a flair of anger. It had been enough to throw the lawyer's attention off Henry and onto his client.

Though Henry made sure to struggle against Caleb and Dante when they had come in to take him away.

"Sorry about the hit, by the way," Henry added for the first time. There was a mark on Matt's jaw, roughly the same spot where Henry was currently feeling pain. "When I realized who Travis was and that I wasn't in uniform, I thought we could use my old cover to our advantage." He managed a grin. "And Gage Coulson wasn't known as the type to *not* resist."

Detective Walker snorted. "You kidding me? It was well worth the hit just to see Suzy here nearly lay you out." Matt turned to the two deputies who hadn't seen the incident. "I mean she hit him so hard *I* almost saw stars."

There was a moment when everyone shared in the humor of what had happened. Even Henry joined in with a little laugh. The truth was he had been impressed with not only her strength, but how quickly Suzy had figured out what was going on. She had been made privy to his background but hadn't known the individuals he'd run into while working.

She'd taken a chance on him and it had paid off.

Which was the reason why the room sobered considerably right after their shared humor ended.

"All hell will be raining down," Suzy repeated, voice hard and cold. "It wasn't an accident, taking down our communications. It was a part of a larger, more menacing plan. One that is run by people, not just one person." She looked to Henry. "I don't know Travis like you do, but am I right in thinking that if he had been in contact with Calvin, he would already have known you were a deputy?"

Henry nodded.

"You probably guessed it already, but Calvin was undercover as Parker Coulson," he explained. "Brother to Gage Coulson, aka my undercover identity. Even if Calvin *had* already met with Travis but, for whatever reason, hadn't given away who I really was, I'm pretty sure Travis would have told me he'd seen my supposedly dead brother. Calvin and I wanted to keep our cover as close to reality as we could when it came to our partnership, so brothers worked out well for us. It was no secret that Parker and Gage were close."

Again, that familiar pain of losing someone who was just like a brother ached in Henry's chest. He glanced across the table at Caleb and Dante. It wasn't a secret, either, that they had also gotten close in their time at the department. Dante had been best man for Caleb's wedding. Partners to best friends to basically brothers.

Henry fought the urge to warn them there was still a chance they didn't know each other at all.

However, projecting his past on them wasn't fair. It also wouldn't do a thing to help their present.

So he continued. "Bottom line, Travis would have told me about Calvin. If only to score some points of gratitude with me. I don't think he *could* have kept it a secret even if he'd wanted to."

"It still doesn't make Calvin's sudden appearance and threat less unsettling," Matt pointed out. "I'm still hard-pressed not to believe they're connected. Maybe this all has something to do with the undercover work you both did in Tennessee?"

Henry had already thought long and hard about that. He'd come up relatively empty-handed. "The last long stint of undercover work that we did before Calvin's death—well, what we thought was Calvin's death— involved us infiltrating a small but growing group of gun runners and drug dealers operating through a recreational ranch in Tennessee. He took a job as part of the security and I was an extra set of hands for the hard labor parts of keeping the ranch going. The task force wasn't sure who the main players were, so we divided and conquered until Calvin got his foot in the door. What we thought was a small operation with maybe twenty men ended up being two *competing* operations vying for the top spot in the area."

"I'm guessing by Travis's reaction that the Richlands were one of the opposing factions," Suzy said.

Henry nodded. "Not that I have a lot of love for Travis—who, by the way, we only knew as Glen—but he was right. The Richland family was a bona fide smorgasbord of awful men and women ready and willing to do awful things. There were many times I wished I could arrest them on the spot just for *talking* about the things they had done." He fisted his hand on top of the table, angry. "But we realized the main aggressor, Arnold Richland, was our golden goose. If we could catch him in the act or tie him to the shipments of guns his people were responsible for, we would potentially stop a mounting gang war before it started. Not to mention keep an influx of unregistered and very dangerous guns off the streets."

"What about the other side? The other faction, they didn't run guns?" Dante was leaning forward, attentive.

Henry was used to other law enforcement being interested when he talked about his undercover work. Especially in Riker County. Their undercover work wasn't as in demand as it had been at his former job.

"They were into drugs, meth and pills mostly," he answered. "But their matriarch, Nora, was trying to change that. She had started with negotiations to try to convince the Richland crew to combine forces. It didn't end well. Which is what brought our attention to the ranch in the first place."

"Sounds like a lot of chaos going on," Suzy commented. "And not the good kind."

"We thought we finally were getting the hang of it." Henry snorted. There was no humor in the sound. "We were wrong.

"The night we thought we finally were going to catch Arnold, his family, and Nora and her cronies in talks with their product in tow, everything went south. Quick. A group of Richland's guys ambushed the task force before they could take position. Didn't hesitate opening fire. It was a domino effect that ended in Nora trying to destroy the evidence and get the heck out of Dodge. Before I knew it, the warehouse around us was engulfed in flames. We were trapped. I lost consciousness before we could find a way out. Next thing I know I'm waking up in the hospital, a member from our team having barely pulled me out before the building was too far gone. He said he never saw Calvin."

"But that was the last time you saw Calvin before today," Matt said, trying to confirm. "That's why you thought he'd died in the fire."

Henry nodded. "That and the fact that one of the Richland men trapped with us shot him three times in the chest before the fire let loose and I passed out."

"Well, that would definitely convince me," Matt said.

Henry tightened his fist.

"But I was wrong," he growled. "Not just about Calvin's death but him in general." A thought Henry hadn't had until that moment finally occurred to him. It was nearly overwhelming, pitting his thoughts squarely between more anger and betrayal. "When I saw Calvin today, he didn't have a burn mark on him."

Henry looked to Suzy, the leader of the group, standing tall and ready at the head of the table. Her expression softened. She'd already made the connection. Still, she'd let him voice it.

"Which means, if Calvin's death was for show and he escaped the building before our guys could get in to grab me, he left me to die there."

A silence swept through the room. Matt looked sympathetic as he broke it. "If he faked his death, then there's a good possibility that he could have tipped off the Richlands in the first place."

Each new theory was a dig to Henry's side. Partly because he hadn't thought of them until now. Partly because, if they were true, he hadn't seen Calvin's true motives back then. He'd been blind.

What did that mean for him now?

How could the people sitting around him trust his judgment?

How could they trust him period?

"People suck sometimes."

They all turned their collective gaze to the open doorway. None other than Cassie Gates looked back at them. More aptly, looked back at him. Her eyes were as fierce as ever. Two green orbs that commanded all his attention and held it without contest. "We can account for a lot of stuff with this job, but at the end of the day, some people just choose to suck."

She took a step farther into the room, unflinchingly unapologetic for interrupting. "And there's not anything we can do about it but get back out there and work hard for those who don't suck. Sure, your partner probably ended up being one of the bad guys. Doesn't mean you stopped being one of the good ones. Okay?"

Henry could get lost in those eyes.

And had done so once before.

"Okay," he answered.

Cassie nodded once, like she'd accomplished what she'd come for, and then turned to Suzy. "To be totally honest, I just eavesdropped most of that conversation," she started. It was a bold move, admitting that to the boss. However, Suzy didn't appear to be angry. Instead she waited for an explanation she must have realized was coming.

Henry was starting to see that normal rules didn't always apply to the family that was the Riker County Sheriff's Department. They really were an all-in-this-together kind of group. "But the door was cracked and… well, I think I have some information that might not be so great."

Suzy motioned to the closest chair.

Henry watched as she sat a little awkwardly, minding her stomach.

A baby boy cradled inside.

Which was why what she said next made his blood boil.

"A man showed up at my house just now." She held up her hand, as if knowing they all were a second away from barraging her with questions. "It wasn't Calvin, but it *was* Michael."

THE ROOM EXPLODED in noise. It made her already twisting nerves knot further. Like wind-whipped hair with no brush strong enough to conquer it. Cassie ran her hands through her own hair. It brought little comfort. She hoped no one notice how her hands had a small shake to them.

"I'm fine," she said, collecting her nerve. "He didn't *do* anything other than talk. I don't know if that had anything to do with me being pregnant or Kristen being there, but he left. I was able to get Detective Ansler on his cell and he said he'd go ahead and notify local PD." Cassie didn't meet anyone's eyes. "Still, it spooked me enough that Kristen drove me here. She's in the break room. I hope that's okay?"

Suzy nodded. Out of Cassie's periphery she saw Henry move forward in his seat, anxious.

"What did he say?" His voice was clipped. Like he was holding back.

Cassie wondered if the others heard the difference. She wondered if there really even was a difference.

Or was she just interpreting his concern for something more?

"What did he want, Cassie?"

She exhaled and fanned her fingers across her stomach. Rubbing it, she felt some sense of comfort as she spoke.

"Honestly, I don't know what he wanted," she admitted. "But he apologized. For the 'runaround' earlier. He said he hadn't thought I would get involved but complimented my driving." She remembered how innocent the conversation had been. Michael had been even-tempered, polite and, unless she had misread him, *sincere*. Then there had been a shift in his stance, his tone, too. "After that he told me that it might be a good idea to get out of town for a few days and visit my parents. Said it would be good for me…and the baby."

This time Cassie chanced a look at Henry. The deputy was strung so tight she would bet she could have played him like an instrument had she wanted. Though she would rather have known the thoughts running through his head.

"Then he got into the same car he was in this morning and left. That's when I called Detective Ansler."

Henry's frown nearly rolled in on itself.

He wasn't the only one.

"He threatened you," Matt said.

Cassie shook her head.

"He seemed genuinely concerned," she admitted.

Henry started to open his mouth, so she hurried to finish the thought. "Which, I know, doesn't make sense, but, honestly, I think it was just a warning."

"One that Henry more or less received himself from Travis Newman." Suzy's voice had gone steely. Analytical. They were dancing around something very real. Something much more ominous than a storm in the distance. Something they didn't fully understand.

But desperately needed to.

Despite his anger, or maybe because of it, Henry was the voice that rang loud, clear and steady throughout the conference room. "We don't know who is pulling the strings, but I think what Travis did was the start of something. Something that's going to hurt. 'The people running this thing got a big plan for everyone here.' I don't think the 'here' Travis meant was about the county, or the town, for that matter. I think he was talking about the sheriff's department. Or maybe the people who run it."

Cassie let out a small gasp.

"Billy," she realized.

Henry nodded.

"I think we're about to have an all-out attack against us," he said. "And what better way to start than by getting the sheriff out of the picture and then taking out our communications?" Henry jabbed his finger down on the table's top, capturing everyone's attention even though it was already on him. "'As soon as it gets dark, all hell will be raining down.'"

Suzy straightened, standing tall.

Tall and angry. "So, whoever they are, they're going to hit us tonight."

It wasn't a question.

## Chapter Twelve

"Are you kidding me?" Suzy said, twenty minutes after their meeting in the conference room had ended.

Henry didn't bother keeping his voice low. There was no point. Not when the department around them was one long stream of bustling noise. "You said it yourself. There's a good chance that the department *will be attacked* tonight! And you want to send me home? I know I'm technically new, but you've seen my résumé, you know what I've done." He let his hands fly around the air in front of him, physically broadcasting his frustration. "You know what I *can* do."

Suzy kept her expression tight and guarded. She was in planning mode. He'd caught her right before she was headed in to giving her troops the battle plan.

The troops he'd been told he wasn't included in.

"Listen, I know you're more than capable of helping, but I think the best way you can do that is by not being in or around the department." She pointed outside her office.

For a moment Henry thought he was being told to leave.

She continued. "Travis Newman would never have talked to us, at least not in time if there really is an attack. He *did* talk to Gage Coulson. What if he isn't the only one who's a part of this who thinks that's who you really are? Every minute you are here, you are further risking us losing the ability to use that if we need to again. As much as I admire and empathize with what you have done and been through, the fact of the matter is that right now the department needs Gage. If it wasn't for him, we wouldn't even have an idea of what might be happening."

Henry ran a hand through his hair. He cursed.

Suzy didn't mind.

"What about Calvin?" he had to ask. "And Michael? I think it's pretty safe to say they both know that Gage was just a cover. What if that's already blown and Travis was just the last to know? Even in the criminal world, there are just some people you don't trust with the important details. For all we know, this could be a giant trap. One you are asking me to leave you all to walk into."

Suzy had been indulging him up until that moment, he realized seconds too late.

"I am not asking you do to anything. I am *ordering* you to leave." She leaned forward, resting her fists on the desktop. It was a power move. One she pulled off well. "If this *is* a trap, then having abled-bodied men and women out there will only help us in the long run. But you're right, Travis may not know whatever plan is out there. Heck, we could all be jumping to one big conclusion. And if that's the case, I'm going to need you to be Gage again to figure out what really is going on. Which is why you're going to leave your uniform off and lie low until we figure out what is and isn't a plan or trap."

Henry didn't speak. He was angry.

Angry that he was effectively being benched.

Angry that the reasoning made sense.

"Is that understood?"

Henry met her gaze and nodded. "But I'm not leaving Cassie's side."

The words came out before he knew he was going to say them. Yet he stood by them, resolute. "Michael knows where she lives, which means Calvin could, too. If he thinks that he can hurt me by hurting her, he could use that. Let me make sure that doesn't happen."

Suzy's eyebrow arched high. "I want to point out that Cassie has showed that she can handle herself. She doesn't need any hero or savior to watch over her. I mean, she did come to your rescue earlier. She's clever, quick and resourceful when she needs to be."

Henry had opened his mouth to protest what he thought she perceived as a request—when he fully planned on doing it with or without permission—when she held up her hand in a stop motion.

"However, today there are a lot of unknown pieces

on this particular chessboard. Ones I don't like. So I'd like to have a few of our own in place. Ones we can control. I am not her keeper, but I will suggest she consider having you around until we know what is or isn't happening."

Suzy was done with the conversation. She grabbed a file on her desk and headed for the door.

"And if she doesn't want me around?"

Chief Deputy Sheriff Simmons didn't so much as hesitate in her response. "Then you do it anyway."

THE SKY WAS the perfect blend of blue and gray, caught somewhere in between calm and dreary. The humidity was less pleasing. It made the air heavy and wet. Uncomfortable and unforgiving mixed with the heat. It fused clothes to skin and tempted all moods into souring.

Not that Cassie's mood needed help in that department.

She cast her gaze away from the sky.

Rain was on the horizon, but it wasn't promised. The change in pressure was pricking at her sinuses. A wicked headache would certainly be in her future. Another problem she'd have to endure.

It was much smaller in comparison to the rest.

At least a headache she understood.

The rest?

Calvin and Michael?

A possible attack against the department?

A man she barely knew with the power to completely and utterly derail her thoughts with ease?

Those were things Cassie was having a harder time wrapping her mind around.

Suzy had made a case for her protection that she had and hadn't appreciated. One that involved the walking conundrum that was wrapped in a pair of mouthwatering jeans. Henry had stood by stoically, like a Southern bodyguard waiting in the wings for her to try her hand at either fight or flight.

Instead she'd fallen somewhere in between.

"He can come home with me, check out the house and hang around while I get some things, but then I'm going to Kristen's for the rest of the afternoon and night," she'd said. "After that he can hang outside in the car if he thinks it's a good idea."

Suzy was pushed for time, but she paused long enough to add in another two cents, even using a nickname she'd heard Cassie call herself from time to time. "Better safe than sorry, baby mama."

Suzy had left then, face grim but ready. Henry's expression was also dark yet alert. He didn't speak as they went to the break room to get Kristen. Which was good for Cassie. Two steps inside the break room and she had a crisis of conscience so severe she didn't speak for a moment.

The department might be attacked that night by a formally deceased undercover cop, a self-proclaimed information peddler, and potentially more unknown faces and motives. Not that Calvin's or Michael's motives were clear.

What did they stand to gain going against the Riker County Sheriff's Department?

What was the point?

Cassie wanted to ask her sister that question, to brainstorm possibilities with her built-in best friend, but what good would that do? Telling Kristen everything that had happened was one thing. Telling her everything that might happen?

One look at Kristen, with her head bent over her phone and brow pulled tight, and Cassie made up her mind.

Her sister, plus her family as a whole, had already been through a lot in the last couple of years. Some of it had been personal; most of it had had to do with the scar that would forever be on Cassie's neck.

The bullet that had almost killed her, shot by a man who had simply missed his original target.

If someone was *actually* trying to target her?

Cassie fanned her fingers across her stomach. Protecting her unborn child.

Trying to keep her nerves from overwhelming her.

Some what-ifs were better left unsaid.

"You okay, Kristen?"

Kristen was startled but recovered with a scowl. "Yeah, but no." She stood, agitated. "Work drama. Apparently the Danvers finally want to look at the Banana

House out in Darby. I asked to reschedule and then Candice swooped in, fangs out."

"Banana House?" Henry asked at their elbow as they moved into the hallway. The department was still bustling from trying to get their communications in order. How would it be when Suzy told them to ready themselves for potential battle?

"It's this yellow monstrosity of a house about an hour from here," Kristen answered. "It's been on the market for three years and this older couple from Florida expressed interest in it a while ago. I've been trying to *gently* push them to look at it and they decided today was the day."

"And Candice is her work nemesis," Cassie added.

"Think of me as Luke Skywalker," Kristen said, spreading her arms out dramatically. "And Candice as Darth Vader, who's determined to steal all my clients out from under my nose."

Henry snorted.

"Before you ask, yes, she's seen all the *Star Wars* movies," Cassie intervened. "She knows she just basically said her nemesis Realtor is her father."

Henry laughed again but didn't say anything as they made it outside. Even out of her periphery, Cassie saw his body tighten. Reality was closing in on them again. The next time they stepped foot in the same parking lot, everything could be different.

Cassie thought about Billy holed up in the hospital.

She rubbed her stomach again.

"You know, Kristen, call the Danvers back and tell them you're on your way." Cassie rallied. She focused on keeping all her fears and worries from her voice.

Still, Kristen started to shake her head. "I'm not leaving you, especially not after that man walked right up to your front porch! Banana house, be damned."

Cassie pushed her thumb back at the deputy close behind them.

"He isn't just here for show," she said matter-of-factly. "He's going to be my shadow for the next few hours, just in case. Nothing but a lot of just sitting around and being bored. Plus, you've already done your due diligence in getting me here."

They stopped next to Kristen's car. Cassie had already made up her mind. She wasn't going to leave with her sister. No, she wanted her out and gone from Carpenter for now if she could swing it.

However, Kristen's jaw was set firm. "Cassie, that man knows where you live. What's to keep him from showing up again? No, I'm not leaving while you willingly go back like you've forgotten that fact."

Cassie opened her mouth, though she didn't know how to respond. Kristen was the only relation she had in the area, and her house was a stone's throw away. Cassie wasn't about to try to stay with friends, especially considering most were her colleagues or either their loved ones. If she *was* a target?

She would never forgive herself for willingly putting her friends and their families in danger.

"She can come stay at my place until you're done."

The certainty and surprise of Henry's baritone sent a wayward shiver of feeling through Cassie. She hoped the smile she threw on covered it.

"Only a few people in the department even know where I'm staying. Not even my brother knows exactly where I've been laying my head. I doubt Michael, or anyone, could track me down easily."

Kristen looked between them, uncertain.

"And if they did?" she asked, protectiveness clearly thronging through her voice.

Henry returned the feeling with some of his own. "Then I'd make sure they got what was coming to them."

It was a promise.

One that Cassie believed with all her being.

One that Kristen seemed to believe in, too.

She nodded, but not before throwing her arms around Cassie.

"I want you to text me every half hour," she said into her ear. "Got it?"

Cassie smiled into Kristen's wild hair. "Got it."

They shared another embrace before Kristen got into her car. Henry stayed at Cassie's elbow, silent, as they watched her drive away. It wasn't until they were sitting inside his personal car that he spoke again. "You don't want to be around her just in case you're a target."

His gaze slid to her throat. Once again the scar at her neck burned. For the first time since she had met the man, Cassie realized there was a chance he had no idea where it had come from. After they'd gotten close, and she believed they were about to get closer, all those months ago, Cassie had almost told him.

But she hadn't wanted his pity.

She hadn't wanted to relive it, either.

Now, though?

Now she found she wanted him to know.

And not just because it would explain the grisly scar, but because it might show him the severity of what could happen when meaningless anger and violence were directed even at the places where they felt the safest.

Cassie slowly touched the circular scar and spoke around the lump forming in her throat. "Before Billy married his wife, she became the target of some really bad people. They didn't play by any rules of decency and targeted Billy and Mara's daughter. While everyone was trying to figure out what was going on, I offered to watch her. We were in the conference room when a shooter took aim at a witness inside the department."

Cassie tapped the scar. The fear of that day threatened to burst through her defenses. She held strong. "The first shot found me instead of the mark. I managed to pull Alexa into a corner and cover her until Billy and Mara could get her to safety. I lost consciousness after that and almost bled out."

Henry's jaw hardened.

His eyes narrowed.

His nostrils flared.

It helped her continue.

"I made it through everything, and I absolutely don't regret helping Billy and Mara. You see, I love them and the rest of the department. They're friends. They're family. But there is one thing I do regret about everything that happened."

"What your family went through," Henry guessed, surprising her.

Nevertheless, he was right.

"They won't say it, but it nearly destroyed my parents. They stayed by my side for months while I recovered. My brothers and sisters weren't far behind. They all tried their best to get me to move away from Riker County, even offering up their homes to me. But I didn't want to move. I've made this place my home. One I want to grow old in. One I want to raise my family in."

She averted her eyes for a second. Was Henry now included in that family? Did he want to be? Cassie sighed and finished her story. "It wasn't until Kristen moved to Carpenter that everyone backed off. If you ask why she moved here, she'll tell you that she wanted a change and had fallen in love with Carpenter when we were young. That she's too self-involved to uproot her life to keep an eye on her baby sister since everyone else is married or has careers that they can't just leave. But the truth is, after I nearly died, something in my family changed and she's had the hardest time dealing with it. I don't think she'll ever leave my side."

She straightened in her seat and cleared her throat.

She had finally made it to her point, even if she hadn't known what it was when she'd started. "People can do awful, awful things sometimes and within the space of a moment everything can change. Whatever it is that Calvin, Michael and whoever else might be out there has planned, I won't let it hurt the ones I love. If that means keeping them in the dark and keeping a low profile? Then so be it. You won't get any resistance from me."

Henry started to speak but Cassie cut him off.

"But I'm here to tell you that I'm not some pregnant damsel in distress," she added, words heated. With them she felt a surge of adrenaline and decisiveness. Cassie looked into the true-blue eyes of a man who had given her the best gift she'd ever received in her entire life and gave him her ultimatum. "Whatever you choose to do in regards to being in my child's life, I will support. If you want to be a part of his life, I will be on board. If you don't want to be a father, then I can make that work, too. But only if you help me do one thing. Help me figure out why Calvin Fitzgerald is in my town, why he wants you dead, and how the sheriff's department plays into it all before anyone else gets hurt. Deal?"

Henry's face was blank. She couldn't read his thoughts let alone any feelings he'd had at her words. It didn't matter. What she needed now was his word.

And she got it.

"Deal."

## Chapter Thirteen

"You're staying *here*?"

Henry pulled into the hotel parking lot and followed it around back, the Eagle in his rearview mirror. Cassie's lips settled into a frown. Even without lipstick they were a luscious red. The same lips he'd gotten acquainted with in the very same hotel he was parking behind.

"I liked it well enough the last time I was here. I figured why roll the dice on trying to find a new one?"

Cassie didn't respond. In fact, after giving her grand speech at the department, she hadn't said a word during the drive over. It wasn't like he had, either. The blonde had a way of throwing him off his game.

First, she'd opened up about the scar he'd always wondered about. That alone had his blood boiling—when everything settled down, he'd make sure to pull that report and read it personally—but then she'd switched gears on him so fast he'd barely been able to keep a straight face.

*If you want to be a part of his life, I will be on board.*

*If you don't want to be a father, then I can make that work, too.*

Just like that, she'd given him a choice. Two, actually. To be in his son's life or not.

Was it that simple?

He knew which way his heart was leaning, but then there his brain was, pulling the other way.

He'd led a dangerous, mostly solitary life for the last several years. One that already had consequences threatening his new home.

*Calvin.*

Henry fisted his hand as he got out of the car. Cassie was right. They needed to figure out the now before he could even think about the future. *That* was his choice. Protecting the beautiful woman a few feet away and the child she was carrying, and stopping whatever Calvin intended to do.

The hotel was a five-story box. No pool, no mints on pillows and a small staff. Nothing fancy. However Henry enjoyed it. Mainly for its proximity to the Eagle and several restaurants and shopping farther down the block. At night the sounds of pleasant chatter rose to his window. It was a far cry from what he'd been used to undercover.

Cassie followed him like she had blinders on. She didn't look at Mike as they passed through the lobby. The potbellied day manager had his favorite classical music station playing from a small Bluetooth speaker underneath the front desk. He gave them a friendly wave, which only Henry returned. Like the staff of the Eagle across the street, Mike made it no secret that he was a fan of local law enforcement. He'd even gotten Henry a deal on his room.

Which Henry realized might have been one of the reasons Cassie's brow was furrowed deeper than her frown. Something that was confirmed when she took one look at the sign across the elevator's closed doors.

"Out of order," she deadpanned. "Does that mean I have to walk up five flights of stairs?"

She placed her palm over her stomach. Her cheeks took on a rosy tint. Henry wasn't sure if it was from the weather or something else.

"I'm not staying in the same room as last time, if that's what you're asking." Memories, hot and sizzling, soft and sweet, all threatened to come back as he thought about Room 504.

*Not the time, Ward*, he thought to himself. A second later he found himself wondering if she was struggling with the same thoughts.

Or, judging by her tone, maybe her memories of their time spent there hadn't been good ones.

*That* was another thought that didn't sit right with him.

"I have a bigger room this time," he said, steering her toward the stairs in the corner of the lobby. "It's a suite on the second floor."

Cassie nodded. He chanced a look her way. The lines across her forehead began to smooth.

"Good. Because if it was on a higher floor I might just stay down here." She made a grunt and kicked out one of her feet. "One perk of pregnancy that has stuck with me has been swollen feet. They're trying to break out of my shoes like a pair of inmates wanting to flee prison."

Henry stifled a laugh.

He had zero experience with pregnant women, but he had a feeling laughing at their pregnancy pains was a big no-no.

So instead he kept quiet and pulled out his key.

The smell of lemon cleaners and fabric softener filled his senses the moment they stepped into the second-floor hallway. Another reason he'd chosen to stay at the hotel while he searched for a place to live was in part how clean the place was. After spending years doing undercover work and staying in less than desirable locales, Henry found how much he valued a well-kept place to rest his head. Not to mention a relatively safe place. The simple layout of one long hallway with rooms off to each side and another stairwell at its end was also a bonus in his eyes.

Hard to be ambushed when you could see everything in one glance.

Room 201 was on the corner and because of that fact gave them three sets of windows instead of the two that all the suites had. The living area had one over the TV and its stand that looked out at the employee parking lot and the offices next door and another on the connecting wall that showed a clear view of the Eagle across the street. The third window from the small but efficient bedroom had the same view. Cassie took a moment to look through each but stopped short of the open door that led to the third. Instead she redirected herself to the couch.

When she looked back up at him, her expression was expectant.

"Now let's talk about Calvin," she said.

Henry caught himself smiling.

"You want anything first?" he asked, motioning to the minifridge next to the TV stand. "All I have is bottled water, but I was thinking about calling in some food to the front." On cue his stomach groaned. He patted it, hitting muscle. "I don't think I've eaten today, to be honest."

Cassie perked up a little. She mimicked his stomach-patting. "I already ate but I'd be lying if I said I couldn't do it again." Her cheeks flushed rosy once more. "Do you think you could call in some pizza?"

He nodded. "Yes, ma'am."

CASSIE DECIDED NOT to push on about Calvin until after their pizza was delivered. In truth her ultimatum had caught even her off guard, especially when she'd been ready to pull the trigger the moment they'd stepped into the hotel suite. Then again, she hadn't been prepared to be back at the scene of the crime, so to speak.

The room might have been plain, small and on a different floor, but Cassie felt like she was surrounded by hot spots of memories. The elevator had been the first one. The pale blue room door had been another.

The bed, with its king-size frame and white linens, was like something someone had stuck a blinking, neon marquee light over with an arrow pointing at its top.

She'd had to sit to ground herself, her thoughts. Her body.

Because, no matter what her mind said about Deputy Henry Ward, her hormones were steadfast in their thoughts about him.

He was a tall drink of sexy.

With and without his clothes on.

Though Cassie found herself almost drooling about the latter. Running her hands over the flat, muscled stomach as it hovered over her. Moaning while his lips caressed the side of her neck, moving down across her exposed skin. Feeling the hardness behind his zipper, pressing against her own desire.

"They said to give them about fifteen," Henry said, coming back into the living area. "Mike will call me down when they get here. I told him I didn't want anyone knowing where I was staying. Old habits, but I guess they're working out for us so far."

Cassie felt the scorching heat flash up her body and into her cheeks. She'd gone and let her hormones get the better of her and, boy, had they done a dang good job! Just remembering the start of their night months ago had put her entire body in a state of lust.

One that was holding even as her brain was shouting that this was a different situation. A different time.

"You okay?" Henry asked before she could even fumble together a response to what he'd said before. Every part of her seemed to be warring between reaching out to the man a few feet from her and the idea of running right out of the hotel and never looking back.

"Oh, yeah, I'm just a little warm." She scrambled for words, standing quickly. "You know I used to be good with the summers here and…well, I'm not anymore. If you excuse me, I think I might go to the bathroom for a moment."

Henry's eyebrow arched and then his expression was covered in concern.

That same concern only started to ignite more fires within her.

She wanted him to hold her. To soothe her. To touch her.

Which was why she nearly ran to the bathroom. Shutting the door with a little too much force, Cassie rounded to the sink and turned the water on high. She splashed the coldness on her face for a good minute.

Yet it barely made a dent in the sheer amount of desire coursing through her.

"Pregnancy hormones," she whispered to herself. "That's all this is. Biological. Normal. That's it."

Her words and rationale did little to settle the swell of her chest. Her heartbeat was starting to gallop just at the thought of Henry's fingers moving along her body, stopping only to tease her. How her nipples had hardened into pearls as his tongue had followed behind, sending her nearly to the brink without even getting to the main event yet.

How the warmth of him had moved against her, both swollen with desire.

How he'd captured her mouth when she bowed up against him, wanting—*needing*—more.

Cassie could still remember how she'd balled fistfuls of the sheets in her hands as he'd pressed against her opening, teasing.

Then, slowly, he'd moved inside enough for them both to feel the beginning of what could be fantastic before pulling back out.

"Not yet," he'd said, voice thrumming low and heavy. Cassie had moved her hands up his biceps and wound them in his hair. She had gotten a good grip and pulled his mouth down to hers, hungry.

It had been a move he clearly hadn't anticipated.

One he couldn't fight, either.

He'd parried her tongue with hers, grabbed her hips and had thrust deep inside her.

Cassie had moaned as Henry's movements slowed. The heat and hardness filled her, pushing her closer and closer to the edge again. When he'd picked up speed, she'd barely been able to keep it together.

Two bodies in want. Feeding off each other's desires. Playing off each other's pleasures.

Then together they'd both let go.

As far as Cassie was concerned, nothing aside from that room had existed that night.

And now?

She looked at her reflection. It was easy to see what she wanted. Just as it was hard to deny the attraction she felt for Henry would still be there with or without pregnancy hormones.

A knock sounded on the door.

The low baritone that had once washed over her naked body soon followed.

"Cassie?"

Her fingers curled around the edges of the sink. She felt her nipples harden beneath her bra.

How could he affect her so strongly?

His voice alone seemed to be tied to every part of her.

Before she could clobber up a response, another knock sounded.

It wasn't on her door, this time it was farther away.

"Turn out the light and stay in there," came Henry's voice. It was harsh. Quick.

It took every feeling of desire, lust and a good deal of the unknown surrounding both to shut them down. Hard.

Cassie flipped the light switch. Darkness enveloped her.

Her heartbeat continued to gallop.

This time it was from fear.

She held her breath, straining to hear. They were probably both overreacting. Maybe the pizza man had been really close? And already had their pizza made and ready within the minute or so it had taken to order?

Cassie's stomach knotted.

Maybe it was someone from the department.

Henry had already said a few had known where he was staying.

Or, maybe, it was Kristen.

Though, with a sinking feeling, Cassie realized they hadn't even told her where they were going other than to some hotel.

Cassie took a step toward the door. She leaned her ear against it, hoping against all hope that her feat was unwarranted. That she was just being silly. That her emotions were all over the place because she was pregnant.

A loud *bang* sounded in the suite. The door shook against her face. Cassie covered the scream that tried to tear itself from her mouth.

She had to use both hands when another sound came through the door.

Something heavy had fallen.

Or someone.

# Chapter Fourteen

The world spun.

Henry fell. The weight of the hotel door pushing him hard to the floor. His head whipped back against it. Spots danced along his vision. He was going to pass out.

The man filling the doorway was breathing in and out like a bull readying to charge. The whites of his eyes were wild and wide, contrasting against his dark clothes and complexion. He had on a pair of hiking boots that had no doubt helped him kick the door right off its hinges. If it had been a newer hotel, he would have had to try a lot harder. As it was, Henry currently had a hunk of aged wood against him.

Which he needed to remedy.

Fast.

"Where is he?" the man roared. "Where is Matt Walker?"

Henry ignored his doubling vision and used his own boots to kick off the fragmented door. He reached for his hip holster, but the man stopped his questioning long enough to see the move. Henry rolled to the side as the

Goliath ran forward and slammed his foot down, right where Henry's head had just been, like he was trying to crush a bug.

Again Henry's head threatened to spiral him into the darkness of unconsciousness but he rallied against it. Adrenaline pumped through his veins. He unbuttoned the clasp of his holster and pulled his gun. Goliath roared again. A meaty fist collided with Henry's jaw. The same one Suzy had already bruised. Bright, hot pain shot across his chin.

"I saw you two together last night," Goliath yelled, swinging his other fist around like an ambidextrous prizefighter. "Where does he live?"

Henry didn't have time to answer his questions. He rolled to his right, avoiding another blow. Whoever the man was, he was determined.

Henry just didn't know what he was more determined about. Crushing him? Or getting answers to his questions?

Either way, Henry wasn't about to take the time to suss it out. He got to his feet and had to do a quick two-step backward, just out of Goliath's raging wingspan.

One thing Henry did know—he was through playing defense.

Using as much power as he could put in his non-dominant fist, he repaid the man in kind for the pain now radiating across his jaw. The hit connected hard. Goliath staggered to the side but didn't fall.

Still, it created space between them and was enough of a window that Henry could use.

He brandished his gun with enough adrenaline backing him that he almost felt like he could take the man on with one hand.

But with Cassie hiding in the bathroom, he didn't want to take any chances. "Freeze or I'll shoot!"

Goliath roared.

And did something Henry hadn't expected.

He did exactly as he was told.

Chest heaving and rage clear in his dark eyes, Goliath looked down his large nose at Henry and obeyed.

"Do you have any weapons on you?" Henry asked, reinforcing his stance. If the man so much as twitched in his direction, he'd take him out. No more chances.

"I *am* the weapon," he said with reverence. There was enough ego to choke a horse.

"Any knives or a gun?" Henry pushed.

The man blew out a snort through his nose. Again, reminiscent of an angry bull. In this instance Henry was the red flag. "Where is Matt Walker?" he asked instead. Malice dripped off each syllable.

Henry didn't understand the question. Or, really, why *he* was being asked and how it fit into breaking down *his* hotel room door. "What's it to you?"

Goliath seemed to be close to bursting at the seams. Pent-up anger mixed with adrenaline and, by the glaze of his eyes, probably narcotics of some kind. Henry recognized that destructive energy. He'd been around it on the ranch undercover. He'd felt it himself once or twice, too.

Whatever was in the man a few feet from him, he wasn't going to hold it in much longer. Gun pointing in his face or not.

Henry was already on thin ice. And only growing heavier with as each second went by.

"He ruined my life," Goliath said. "I want to repay him for that."

"And why are you here?" Henry couldn't resist asking.

Goliath's eyes trailed over his shoulder to the window behind him. Henry wasn't about to turn his back on the man, though.

"I can't find him. He doesn't live in the same house he used to. You were with him yesterday, but I couldn't follow you. So you know where he lives. Where he is now." He glanced back at Henry like he was a mild annoyance. "And it's almost time for—"

"You boys sure do talk a lot."

For one wild moment Henry thought it was Cassie who interrupted. But the woman who sashayed through the open door and around Goliath was definitely not the woman he'd had on his mind the last several months.

Henry ball-parked her age in the mid to late twenties. He didn't recognize her. Tall, thin and sneering, she had jet-black hair, braided in pigtails, wore a black tank top that showed her pierced belly button and a pair of dark jeans that were so tight they left little to the imagination. Not that Henry cared about any of that. What he was pinpoint focused on was the shotgun she held steady in her hands.

He met her aim with his own. She didn't flinch.

Instead she *tsk*ed at him.

"I'm quick," she said, her sneer widening. "And even if I'm not…"

Movement caught his eye but not his aim as another unknown entered the room. This time it was a man. Compared to the threat that Goliath and the woman obviously presented, he did little to compare. Short and wiry, he was sweating openly. Nervous. The handgun he moved in Henry's direction shook.

"Jason may be slightly useless, but he *does* know how to pull a trigger," she added.

If Jason was offended, he didn't show it.

Henry kept his aim on the woman.

Three against one.

He should have taken out Goliath when he'd had the chance.

"So how's this going to play out?" Henry kept his voice even. Calm. He aimed the question at the woman. She seemed to be the one in charge. "You threaten to kill me to get to Matt?"

Goliath actually smiled. Henry was talking his language now.

The woman, however, wasn't. She laughed.

"I don't care about Detective Walker," she clarified. "In fact, I don't care about you, either. I just need you to be here and be still for a little while. So, if you'd please, put your gun down before I let Kevin here rip you from limb to limb like he seems to want to."

Goliath, apparently named Kevin, swung his head around, already biting his words off in anger. "He said I could have Matt. This guy knows where he is. So he's mine."

The woman wasn't amused. Her sneer wiped off, replaced by thinly veiled disgust. "I run things here. He stays here *and* alive until I say." She snorted. "You shouldn't have waited so long to get your shit together, Kevin. You should have already done your homework like everyone else. Not my fault you're an idiot."

Kevin rounded on the woman so fast that Henry barely had time to clear the shotgun blast she sent into the big man's chest. Blood and bone and everything in between exploded along with sound through the small area. The woman might have been ready to shoot, but she hadn't braced herself properly. She flew backward into the small dining set in the corner next to the door. Kevin went in the opposite direction.

Henry's ears rang with the shot, but he wasn't about to waste his opening. He turned his gun toward Jason. The man might have been nervous, but his boss had been right. He did know how to pull a trigger. He shot at Henry but missed, hand shaking like a leaf.

Henry could have ended him right there, but he refused to return fire. Not when his angle was all off. If he missed the man or the bullet went straight through him, its trajectory would be pointed straight at the bathroom. He wasn't about to chance Cassie or his son.

His son.

The thought flashed across his mind with such an intense feeling of protectiveness that it rallied Henry even more. He knew then that, no matter what, he'd take on anyone and anything to keep his child safe.

Rushing the small man who looked like he was about to unravel? A no-brainer.

Henry closed the space between them before Jason could get another shot off. He grabbed his wrist and pulled up hard. The man let out a cry and dropped his gun but not before Henry used the butt of his service weapon to strengthen his next blow. The hit dazed the man. He fell to his knees. Henry drew back and landed a knock-out hit. Jason crumpled to the floor with a whimper.

"Ah!"

Henry turned in time to see the shotgun discarded on the floor in the corner. The woman who had been wielding it, however, was not. With a twisted face filled with violence, she was on him within seconds. This time she was swinging a knife. He yelled as it sliced into his shoulder.

"I…can't…kill…you," she grunted against him as he grabbed the hilt of the knife, keeping it from going in any farther. "But… I…can…*hurt you*!"

She kicked out and hit him in the groin. He brought

his gun up to her stomach, but she used another move he hadn't anticipated against him.

With a wild cry she head-butted him.

Pain blossomed across his nose as blood instantly rushed out. The gun in his hand hit the floor, but he wasn't going to let the crazed woman get the better of him. He used his free shoulder and pushed her off him enough to get room to land a kick. It pushed her small frame backward and to the floor.

Henry bent to get his gun, but the woman recoiled like a gold-medaled gymnast. Maybe Kevin hadn't been the only one on something. If he didn't get her under control soon—

A gunshot ran out once again in the suite. The woman fell back once more on the carpet. This time she didn't spring back up. Instead she cried out, cradling her arm.

Henry laced his fingers around his service weapon and turned to take on whoever the new player was. It wasn't like there seemed to be honor among the group so far.

But this time Henry did recognize the shooter.

Cassie stood in a nearly perfect stance, gun held firmly and eyes set on her target.

"You come at him again and I'll prove to you that I was aiming to hit your arm," she said. Not a waver or a break in her voice. "Then I'll aim for something else."

"You've *got* to be kidding me," the woman said in response. Though she didn't make an attempt to move

again. "Damn, Henry! You had a pregnant lady waiting in the wings as backup. I didn't see that coming."
Despite her precarious situation, she laughed. Henry
grabbed the knife in his shoulder and pulled it out. He
tossed it behind him, angry.

"Who do you work for?" he asked, not caring how
cliché it sounded.

The woman clenched her upper arm. Blood pushed
out between her fingers. Still she kept her smile. "Don't
tell me you've already forgotten about your partner,
Deputy. Because I'll tell you what, he hasn't forgotten
about you." She nodded to the dead body she'd created
in the middle of the room. "All of this is really for you."

Thunder rumbled in the distance. The light in the
room had dimmed since Kevin kicked down the door.
It only added to a rise of foreboding in Henry's stomach. What was going on? What was Calvin's game?

"I don't understand," he admitted. "How is any of
this for me? How is finding Matt part of it?"

The woman laughed. This time she flinched at the
movement. "That was Kevin's target. *His* chance at revenge." She shrugged, flinching again. "You aren't the
only one who's stepped on some toes during your career."

Another crash of thunder sounded. Closer.

She turned toward the window.

Henry chanced a glance out, too.

A blanket of clouds darkened the sky above the Eagle
and the town behind it. More menacing than the earlier

flash storm that had popped up. By the looks of it, this one had staying power.

That was when it clicked.

Henry's blood ran cold.

"'As soon as it gets dark, all hell will rain down,'" he said, repeating what Travis had said in the interrogation room. The woman turned to him, lips already curving up into a smile. "You weren't waiting for the night. You were waiting for a storm."

"That's how all this is really for you," she said, positively radiating some kind of sick satisfaction. It was unsettling an already anxious feeling, pulling his muscles tight in anticipation. "He said this would be your perfect nightmare."

Lightning flashed.

Henry backed away from the woman and moved closer to Cassie, never taking his eyes off the former. "Cassie, there's a flashlight in the top drawer in the nightstand," he rasped. "Get it. Now."

Henry sensed Cassie's hesitation. Judging by the woman's smile, they might not be able to afford it.

"Ah, there it is," she cooed. "Now you know what happens next." She turned her head to face the window. As if she didn't have a care in the world. "Out there is about to get crazy. Don't say I didn't try to protect you, Deputy Ward."

Henry heard the drawer in the next room open. Cassie had to have been maybe five steps behind him. It was too far away.

Another boom lightly shook the glass in the windows. This time it wasn't thunder.

Henry watched helplessly as the town of Carpenter's power slowly blinked out.

"Cassie?" He tried, but it was too late.

The lights didn't even flicker. They all just went out.

## Chapter Fifteen

The AC whirled as it shut down. The air in the suite went from cool to stale in what felt like one second flat. It was such a loud silence by contrast that Cassie stalled by the edge of the bed. What had been the beginning of a storm in the distance was now a darkness that reached through the windows and created the void she had been thrown into.

The adrenaline high she'd taken advantage of after hearing Henry cry out in pain was dropping off.

Suddenly she felt like a child again, terrified of the darkness.

"Cassie."

She couldn't see him, but Henry's voice was enough to bring her out of the fear clinching her chest like a vise. She remembered the weight in her hand. The flashlight was small but illuminated her immediate area. Enough that she saw Henry's concern clearly.

Without being asked Cassie tossed the light over. He was fast to turn it on the woman who had attacked him. She hadn't moved from her spot. She was still smiling, too.

It sent a chill down Cassie's spine.

"The more you shine that thing on me, the faster he'll end up finding you," the woman said, almost coyly. Like she was trying to flirt with Henry. Cassie didn't like it for several reasons.

"Cassie, can you keep a gun on her while I get my cuffs?"

Henry's entire demeanor was hard. He was channeling the law right now.

In answer Cassie lifted her gun and braced her feet apart again. She knew how to shoot and not just because she worked in a sheriff's department. Three Christmases ago, her eldest brother, Davie, had given each of his sisters shooting lessons and paid for their classes to get licenses to carry. She'd have to make sure to thank him again.

Henry propped the flashlight on the coffee table so the woman was in the spotlight and made quick work of cuffing her to a wooden leg of the entertainment cabinet. He left her wounded arm alone and free. Not that it would do much good. If she wanted to escape she'd have to flip the cabinet and the TV. Cassie doubted she could manage it at the awkward angle she was sitting on the floor.

But if she did, at least they'd hear it and have a heads-up.

The woman stayed quiet during the deed and didn't

try to resist. It somehow made Cassie even more nervous than if she had tried. The woman was too confident, which made everything she'd said to Henry in the last few minutes even more terrifying.

Calvin, and who knew who else, was coming.

Could she shoot him, too?

Cassie's stomach twisted. She'd never shot someone before. She was a dispatcher, for heaven's sake. The most action she'd seen was when *she* had gotten shot.

Suddenly the rest of the hotel suite started to come into focus around the beam of light. The shadows of two bodies were in front of her. One unconscious, one dead. The scent of copper filled the air. Cassie felt light-headed.

Not copper.

Blood.

"I—I need to leave." Even to her own ears she heard her voice break. The silence before and after made the fragility of it even more noticeable. She wasn't the same woman who had just shot someone in the arm.

Both Henry and the woman turned to look at her. Only one was smirking.

"I think she just realized she's standing in Kevin's blood and guts," the woman said. "Might want to make sure if she passes out to do it backward and not forward."

Cassie wanted to reply with something witty but the woman was right. She *was* about to pass out. Her vision started to tunnel. Without the flashlight's beam she might not have noticed the difference. A cold sweat broke out all over her body.

Henry was at her side in a flash, picking up the flashlight in the process. Its bouncing beam did little to help her attempt to calm down.

"Why don't you go back into the bathroom?" he urged. "I'll call in to the department and come and get you when someone gets here."

He tried to gently nudge her back into the closet-size bathroom. It caused an almost overwhelming sense of anxiety within her.

"I don't want to be trapped in there again," she whispered. "It's too small. It feels like being backed into a corner." She reached out and took his forearm. Warmth spread between them. It helped anchor her thoughts. "And I already tried to get hold of someone while I was in there. No one answered." She squeezed his arm as dread began to pool in her stomach. *"No one."*

The woman laughed.

"You're all cut off now, honey," she said. "Now all we have is the fun."

Henry stiffened. The unmistakable sounds of voices shouting somewhere in the building floated through the open door.

"Don't look so surprised. I might not be a top dog, but one of them sure does like me."

"Oh, God, they're coming for her," Cassie related. That was why the woman wasn't afraid. Which meant she thought Henry and Cassie were no match. Cassie thought about her unborn child. "What do we do?"

Henry took less time to contemplate. He moved the beam over the woman's face one more time. When he spoke, his voice was low and thick with anger. "Tell Calvin only children play games."

Then he took Cassie by the hand and pulled her along with him into the hallway. He barely took a beat before cutting to the right and running. The flashlight beam did little to quell the fear of the dark around them. Whoever had been shouting in the lobby was now pounding up the stairwell behind them.

Luckily, they weren't going to be seen.

Henry opened the door to the second set of stairs and ushered her inside. This time he stopped for a moment, listening. Cassie tried to mimic him, but her heart was hammering against her rib cage so hard she wasn't sure if that was what she was hearing or thunder in the distance.

"The Eagle," he whispered when he was satisfied with what he did or didn't hear. "Would Hawk have guns there?"

Cassie was surprised he knew the bar owner's nickname, but she answered. "Yes, and he'd be ready to shoot them."

Henry readjusted the flashlight and started down the stairs, careful not to pull her too much. Which was good; she was starting to get really winded. Since she'd found out she was pregnant, she'd been doing prenatal yoga and other exercises to keep her in shape the best she could, but running for her life hadn't been on the recommended list of daily activities.

Another roar of thunder shook the building. This time the rain wasn't far behind. Henry swore under his breath but kept on. When they got to the door leading out, however, he turned to face her full-on for the first time. As he aimed the flashlight down between them, Cassie could barely make out the blue of his eyes as shadows danced across his face.

"Do you trust me?"

It was such an odd question. Simple yet in no way simple. One yes or no answer that fundamentally changed how their relationship would work.

Did Cassie trust Henry Ward?

The man who had stolen her heart with no obvious plan to return it.

The man who had said nothing of the child they shared in her stomach.

The man who she'd known less than a handful of days and yet felt a connection with unlike any other she'd felt before.

Cassie already knew the answer. "I do."

"Good. Because I have a plan. One that you might not like."

THE SIDE DOOR led out to a covered walkway that looped around the back of the hotel. Since the front of the building began a foot from the sidewalk, anyone checking in used the drive there instead. Which meant as soon as they cleared the awning they were currently under, they'd be pummeled by the rain.

And lose most of their already limited visibility.

"Are you okay to run again?" Henry asked. There was no point trying to whisper when Mother Nature was all-out yelling around them. Thunder and lightning sparred in the sky. Too close for comfort. Just like Calvin's lackeys inside.

Caught between a rock and a hard place?

More like forced between a hard place and a hard place.

In the dark.

"Yeah, but I don't think I can go that fast." Cassie held her belly in one hand and her gun in the other. It was a sight that unsettled him yet made him feel a twinge of pride. Not only had she probably saved his life, she'd done it seven months' pregnant to boot.

"I'm going to let you go first just in case they decide to pop up behind us, okay?"

Cassie nodded. Another boom of thunder drew her frown in on itself. She reached out and took the flashlight from him. The storm was heavy but not nasty. Not yet, anyway. Without the streetlamps, the only light they had to pull from was the sky itself, and that was dim at best. If Henry hadn't been comfortable with the Eagle, he might not have attempted the trip. He reached out and took Cassie's shoulder. Together they moved out and through the rain.

Cassie went faster than he expected but did her due diligence before crossing each street lane. The Eagle didn't get popular until around seven and the hotel was in one of its slower months. Not to mention, as far as he could tell, Carpenter had gone lights out. If anyone was in the hotel, he hoped they were sticking to their rooms after hearing the gunshots. He also hoped that Mike the manager was still alive. Henry had a feeling the man wouldn't have let the woman and her goons upstairs without a fight.

Now the question was if Hawk the bar owner was in his bar and would willingly help.

They made it to the front double doors without any people or cars coming at them. The bar was dark, like the rest of the block save for the small light in Cassie's hand. She waved it across the glass. Henry stopped her before she opened the door.

"If anything goes sideways, I want you to run and hide," he said, angling down so his mouth was next to her ear. The rain had only intensified the smell of her shampoo. Citrus and spice. An intoxicating mixture against the wet skin of a beautiful woman. "Okay, Cassie?"

She nodded against the rain, hair darkening as it grew more wet, and let Henry pull her behind him. She kept the flashlight over his shoulder as they moved inside. Henry kept his gun low but wasn't for a second going to let them be ambushed.

*Again.*

Like the hotel suite, the inside of the Eagle was so quiet it was nearly deafening. The air was still cool from the AC but felt stiff in the open, dark space. Cassie swept her light ahead and across the bar. No one was behind it or at any of the tables or booths. The main room was empty.

"The door was unlocked," Cassie said, this time at his ear. Without the rain beating down on them, she went back to a worried whisper. "Hawk has to be in the back."

Henry turned and put his finger to his lips. Cassie fell silent, eyes widening. He would bet Hawk *was* in the back. It was just his condition Henry was concerned about. What if the woman and her goons had looked for him at the Eagle first?

He walked Cassie to the corner, out of view from the windows if the lights did come back on, and pressed his fingers to his lips one more time to push his point home again. If he could, Henry wanted to keep Cassie a secret like he had done in the hotel room. There were too many unknown variables. He couldn't guarantee her safety if all hell hit the fan. It was that thought alone that had made up his mind to run across the street in the first place.

Cassie handed the flashlight to him. He put the small light in his mouth and pulled out his gun. He moved as quietly as his wet boots would allow across the hardwood until he was behind the bar at a door that led into the kitchen.

No one jumped out or said anything. The silence from the main room stretched all the way past the grill and cooler out into another door that led to a small hallway. Henry tilted to look toward the front of the building. The hallway ran to the front, passing two small bathrooms. He moved his chin around to face the other end. The beam lit up two doors. One led, he assumed, to the back alley. If he had to guess, the other led to the office. The door was open.

The sound of rain pelting the one-story building intensified. Henry moved down the hall, muscles coiling in anticipation. His brother's voice echoed through his head.

*You are good at a lot of things, Henry, but stealth isn't your strong suit.*

Hopefully he'd gotten better since Garrett had made the comment. Though the moment he swung around the open doorway, gun and flashlight high, he realized that maybe his brother was still right.

"Don't move or I'll blast a hole through your chest," the man said, eyes narrowing in the light.

For what felt like the umpteenth time in the last two days, someone had a gun pointing at Henry.

And, boy, was it getting old fast!

## *Chapter Sixteen*

Henry lowered his gun slowly. With his free hand he took the flashlight from his mouth, also slowly. The man nicknamed Hawk had been waiting in the dark for him. He surely wasn't going to loosen his stance any time soon. Better not to spook him.

"My name's Henry Ward," he started, keeping the flashlight pointed ahead. "I'm the new deputy at the sheriff's department. I was in here several months ago and—"

"And helped get Gary to his cab in exchange for a drink," he interrupted gruffly. "I'm bald, not dumb. Why are you here in my business, lurking around with your gun out?"

Henry motioned toward the hallway. He needed to be honest. If the sheriff and the department seemed to trust the bartender, then he would, too. Especially considering his own track record with apparently misplacing trust. "I've been staying across the road. A few minutes ago we were ambushed by three perps before the lights went out. One's dead and the other two were incapacitated, but more came into the building. I didn't want to take any chances of a shoot-out, since my friend's pregnant. I thought she'd stand a better chance being here until things got sorted out."

Hawk's demeanor barely shifted. He didn't lower his gun but his eyes went over Henry's shoulder. "Who's your friend?"

"Cassie Gates."

It was like her name was the magic word. The hardened man across from Henry lowered his gun and took up a look of such great concern that he felt a shot of adrenaline go through him.

"Is Cassie okay?" Hawk asked, bending to pick up something.

Henry was relieved to see it was a camping lantern. A soft fluorescent light flooded the room. It was small but powerful. "She could probably use a place to rest, but I think she's okay."

Henry stepped into the hallway and they started back to the front.

"You know, I thought I heard a few shots, but with the weather, I chalked it up to thunder," Hawk said, trailing behind him. "Then my cell phone lost service and the lights went out. Knew it was trouble."

"It was intentional." Henry gritted out the words. Anger flared hot in his stomach. Calvin had done it. Or gotten someone to do it for him. Either way, this was him.

And he would pay.

"I figured as much. I don't think the storm is the only thing that's come into town angry."

Henry walked into the main room as a shock of lightning lit up the space. Cassie stood from the corner booth he'd set her next to.

"I found Hawk," he was quick to say. "He's okay, and you were right, he is ready to do some shooting if needed."

Hank held up the lantern long enough for Cassie to cross the room. Henry watched the front windows and door.

"I locked the front door," she said, getting a quick hug from the bartender. "I hope that's okay, Hawk."

"Sounds good to me. It might be better if we pretend we're not home right now, anyways."

Henry nodded.

He didn't want Cassie as exposed as he felt they were just standing around. The rain was still falling in heavy sheets, but if there was a chance Hawk's lantern could still be seen from the street, he wanted to make sure they were at least in a different room.

"Actually, do you have some water I could have? I know I'm drenched, but I also haven't run around like that in a while."

"Sure thing. I have some bottles in the kitchen. Then I think I have some hand towels in the storage room. Might not do the trick, but they'll help."

Henry wanted to be the one who got her water and dried her off. He wanted to be the one who sat next to her and asked if she *really was* okay. But if Calvin was gunning for him, then they weren't safe.

*She* wasn't safe.

Their son wasn't safe.

"I'm going to stay here," he declared, eyes never leaving the darkness outside the door and windows.

Henry felt Cassie hesitate even if he couldn't see her.

"You think they know we came over here?" Cassie asked.

"There's a plan everyone seems to be following. One that I don't fully understand yet. I can't guess at their moves because I don't know their full motives."

"The big guy wanted to hurt Matt, not you," Cassie offered. "But the woman wanted to keep you in that room. She wanted to keep you safe."

Henry nodded. He didn't know if either could see it outside their circle of light.

"Two different agendas, a town-wide blackout and somewhere out there Calvin is up to no good." Henry felt his nostrils flare, anger burning through him again. "It's hard to guess at what happens next when you're still hung up on what's happening now."

Hawk grunted in, what Henry guessed, was agreement. Cassie didn't say a word. The two walked back to the kitchen. Henry turned off his flashlight and set it on the bar in front of him. Complete darkness washed over the room.

Henry didn't want to admit it, but Calvin being hot on his heels was bad, bad news. The man wasn't just smart, he was clever. But what was worse came from the fact that he had always been a man able to adapt. He thought as quickly on his feet as Henry did. It had been one of the reasons they had been paired up and sent undercover in the first place. If Calvin really was pulling the strings, he might pull his puppets right on over to the Eagle.

Because that was where Calvin would have gone if he had a pregnant woman he was protecting. At least, the old Calvin would have.

Was he the same person now?

Had Henry just been blind?

He balled his fists on the bar top. The same one he'd been sitting at when he'd first heard the honeyed voice that was Cassie Gates.

If he'd only known what he knew now…

…He still would have walked over to her sister and pretended he was her date.

Another surprising revelation.

One that was short-lived.

Lighting flashed outside. Then it flashed again.

Henry stiffened.

It wasn't lightning.

Two beams of light strobed in front of the building, getting closer.

Had the goons already figured out where they'd gone?

Henry ducked low and hurried through the door to the kitchen.

"Hawk, lights out," he hissed, rushing to Cassie's side. He took her hand as the bar owner followed instruction without question.

"This is getting old," Cassie muttered.

Hawk beat them to the office and picked up his gun. He turned the lantern back on, low, and put it in the corner. Henry directed Cassie to a chair next to it.

"If that woman is with them, she made it pretty clear that Calvin wanted you alive," she said. "That's good, right?"

"No, it's not."

In the low light Cassie's brow turned in on itself.

He didn't like the explanation he gave. "She didn't say anything about keeping you alive."

CASSIE LET HIS words sink in.

He was right.

She hadn't mentioned keeping her or *anyone* else alive.

No, Calvin had wanted Henry, and Henry alone.

Cassie rubbed her stomach as she watched Hawk and Henry readying their weapons. They were talking quickly, quietly. Tackling what-ifs and bottom lines, she was sure.

She felt useless sitting there but wasn't about to argue. She might have spent the last twenty minutes or so being heroic and ready for action, but the truth was, she was exhausted. Adrenaline surge after adrenaline surge and being soaked from head to toe, she couldn't ignore the fact that she was seven months' pregnant. She couldn't keep up the pace of running for her life. It wasn't good for her or the baby.

"Henry," she called out when it appeared to be go-time. Even in the low light Cassie marveled at how attractive he was. Built for strength, molded by conviction. Sharp angles, soft lips. A storm of a different nature swirling in his eyes. The same eyes that held all of her attention in his gaze. "Be careful. Both of you."

Hawk dipped his head in acceptance of the order. Henry didn't. Instead he issued his own back at her.

"Shoot anyone who comes through this door that isn't us."

And then they took his small light and shut the door behind them.

Cassie blew out a long, low breath, trying to steady her nerves. She grabbed her gun and prayed she wouldn't have to use it again. Last time had been enough to last the rest of her days.

The rain hadn't lessened its onslaught against the roof above. It made it impossible to hear what was going on in the other room.

Maybe nothing would happen.

Maybe Henry was overreacting or trying his best to be cautious.

A warmth in her chest started to expand as she thought of the man taking her hand earlier.

He was doing his hardest to keep her and their child safe.

Did that mean he wanted to be in their life?

Or was he just doing his job as an officer of the law?

Like she was going through déjà vu, a sound in the other room cut off all current lines of thought.

However, this time Cassie could place it.

Someone had shattered glass.

Cassie pulled her gun up. She might be cold, tired and worried, but she wasn't about to let anyone harm her or her child.

THE DARKNESS BETWEEN Henry and Hawk was still thick, but two flashlights were eating up the space on the other side of the bar behind them. Heavy shoes crunched over the broken glass that had once taken up the top half of the front door. Now the feet squeaked along the middle of the room as two perpetrators surveyed the space around them.

Henry might not have been the king of stealth, but neither were the people behind them. After their lights could be seen moving to the kitchen door and the hallway, they had no problem talking to one another.

Loudly.

"Don't look like anyone's here," a deep voice grumbled.

"Yeah, they would have come out by now," another answered. Also male. Henry recognized neither. "Baldy would have already been in our faces if he was here, that's for sure."

"So what you wanna do?"

There was a pause as the other must have been thinking.

Henry couldn't see the bar owner next to him but knew he was ready to start the fight as soon as the signal was given.

"Well, I'm not about to go tell Paula we didn't search the whole place. She's already pissed enough with the bullet in her arm."

The other man agreed with a "Humph."

Henry reached out and touched Hawk's elbow. He didn't wait for a response. Taking a beer glass from behind him, Henry started to slowly stand, readying to throw it as far away from them as possible. It would be the distraction that would get them the upper hand.

Henry arced back, still hidden in the dark while the men's flashlights kept on the hallway ahead of them, and felt his muscles tighten as he focused on mentally picturing the spot in the corner he wanted to hit.

Then, just like that, the bar's overhead lights cut on.

The pumped-up alternate rock from the stereo, some sports game on the overhead TV and the building whirl of the AC unit were all background noise as two armed men stood staring at Henry and his beer glass.

"Well, this is awkward," Henry stated.

Henry followed through with his plan and threw the glass hard. Both men danced away from it, but only one took a shot while doing it. The bullet embedded somewhere over the pool tables to the left of the bar. The beer glass shattered and the second man readied to shoot his own gun.

Hawk was faster.

He shot the second man in the leg while Henry made sure the first didn't get any more ideas. Much like Cassie had done with the woman, named Paula according to the men a few feet from him, Henry clipped the first man.

He yelled out in pain and dropped his weapon.

"Drop yours or I'll shoot again," Hawk ordered.

The man was slower than his friend to fall, but he did lower his gun long enough to slump to the floor, cussing.

"Push the guns away," Henry yelled. "Both of them."

The order did the trick.

Both men kicked and slid their guns away, the first man whimpering as he did so. The second kept to cussing.

Henry and Hawk worked quickly. They substituted plastic zip ties from behind the counter for cuffs. Soon both men were restrained.

"Nice job, Baldy," Henry joked. Hawk snorted. "Now let's see if we can't get hold of someone at the department."

The man shot in the leg spit to the side, earning a scowl from Hawk. Then he bit off some laughter.

Henry didn't like what he had to say.

Not one bit.

"Pretty sure they ain't coming," he said too calmly. Too confidently. "They got their own problems right now."

## Chapter Seventeen

The power had been out for fifteen minutes.

In that time the Riker County Sheriff's Department waited. With their communications already dicey and the power gone, they were ready for an attack.

It never came.

At least, not where expected.

Henry touched the bandage the ER nurse had put over the knife wound in his shoulder. It didn't hurt. Then he felt his nose. Swollen, bruised, but not broken. It hurt, but nothing could compare to what he was currently feeling.

He wasn't angry.

He was furious.

He wasn't the only one.

Suzy threw her fist into the side of the vending machine Henry had positioned himself next to. It made a loud bang but didn't draw anyone's attention but his. Everyone else was busy bustling around. The backup generators had kicked on in the hospital, but because the rest of the town had been dark, there had been an influx of new patients. Some car accidents, a few self-defense incidents when a couple of geniuses got the idea to try to loot some local stores, and then some patients already in-house who'd had trouble before the backup generators could take over.

Billy had been one of the latter. He'd been in surgery after a complication had arisen around lunch. It had almost cost him his life, but the doctor had been fast on her feet.

But that still wasn't why Suzy was so mad.

"They never wanted us," she said, rage spilling out. She ran her hands through her hair and then down her face. "My God, we were so worried about them hitting us and then they went after *our families*."

It wasn't new information to Henry. After they'd gotten a call through to the department, one of the deputies had told him everything. Said how those who hadn't lost their cell signals because of the downed power had started to get calls from the outside world. One where their families were being attacked.

Four hours had gone by since then. In that time they'd found out that Caleb's house had been broken into and his wife had been attacked. The man had tried to get her to his car, but their dog had attacked, giving her time to run and hide. She had gotten stitches but was safely upstairs now.

Others who had been targeted but managed to escape or fight back had been Suzy's mother, Dante Mills's niece, Detective Ansler's brother and Captain Jones's father. All attackers had been since identified as men and women who Caleb, Dante, Ansler and Jones had directly affected by way of arrest, prison sentence or either a family member being arrested or sentenced.

"An eye for an eye," Alyssa's attacker had said while trying to put her in his car.

However, even though that had been the end of the attacks, the main reason everyone was on edge had to do with Matt's fiancée, Maggie.

Even though Goliath had been killed, she'd still been targeted and taken from her home. Her young son had been with her. She'd fought tooth and nail to free him before the man had managed to put her in the trunk and drive off.

Currently the boy was in the room across the hall with a broken arm, Suzy's mother keeping him company.

Maggie had simply disappeared.

"What's the plan now?" he asked, trying to focus her anger.

"Local FBI have integrated into this madness and are helping to look for the people behind this, Maggie's attacker included. The local chief of police is covering the department while the rest of us are trying to get a hold on the situation. Once I go check on Billy and Mara, I'm heading back out there to meet up with Matt. We brought out our reserve deputies to help Ansler try to chase down the people we know are already tied up in this."

The stress Suzy carried wasn't just in her shoulders, it was everywhere. "I'm sheriff for less than two days and the department has been crippled, our families have been targeted and the entire town is put out of commission." She held up her hand to stop his attempt to comfort her. Which he was ready to do, since it was *his* fault that this had happened. He'd already told her everything he'd learned since the hotel room, namely that Calvin had most likely orchestrated the blackout and Paula had been sent to keep him out of harm's way.

Even though that in itself was confusing. If Calvin had recruited a group of angry people looking for revenge on the department, then why would they try to target Henry?

It was one of many questions they'd all had.

But there was no time to sit back and wonder.

"What's happened has happened," Suzy continued. "Now we need to focus on making sure we get Maggie back and bring our perps in. And make sure if another strike happens, we're ready." She pulled something out of her pocket.

Henry was surprised to see it was a key.

"You seem to be an extra-shiny target, which now includes Cassie. If Calvin wants to use Carpenter as his own personal chessboard, then I'm done playing. It's time to take a few pieces off the board altogether."

THE RAIN BARRELED on throughout the night. It only started to taper off once they had driven over the town line, through the city of Kipsy and finally into Bates Hill.

"It's the smallest town in the county," Cassie reported. Her voice came out tired, worried.

Henry knew both feelings well. The old him wouldn't have left Carpenter at all. Not when one of their own was hunting the man who had taken his loved one. Not when they might be subjected to another attack.

Then Cassie would let out a soft sigh or rub her stomach and Henry would remember that there *was* a new him. One who had a woman and unborn child to protect. It was the least he could do, since now, because of him, the off-her-rocker woman, Paula, had seen them together.

The men who Henry and Hawk had taken at the bar had only reiterated two facts before shutting their mouths entirely.

One, that Paula had been shot.

Two, that a pregnant lady named Cassie had been the one who shot her.

Once backup had arrived, Henry had gone through the hotel with them before being taken to the hospital. Mike the manager had indeed put up a fight but was still alive, albeit in need of medical care. Jason, the nervous man who had come in with Paula, had still been unconscious in the suite and Goliath had been just as dead as ever.

Paula and the cuffs were gone. The few guests staying at the hotel hadn't seen her or anyone else come or go from the second floor when the lights came back on.

It was the only reason Henry had agreed to, once again, trying to sit out and hide. Though, this time, he hoped it would actually work. He'd kept his eyes on their surroundings, looking for a tail. He still didn't know how Paula and her lackeys had found them so quickly at the hotel.

Unless they'd gone through his cell phone. It had been new and almost no information had been in it, but, still, maybe Calvin had looked at the recent calls and connected it to the hotel. Then Paula had staked him out? And Goliath had, too?

Henry ground his teeth at the thought.

What madness had he brought with him to Riker County?

"Bates Hill might be small, but it's really come a long way in the last decade or so," Kristen piped up from the back seat. When Henry had told Cassie the plan, she'd refused to go anywhere without her sister, especially since Michael had seen them together.

Kristen had driven to the hospital and as soon as she'd gotten into his car, Cassie had told her everything. This was the first time she'd spoken since Kipsy. "A certain, handsome-as-all-get-out resident millionaire has been helping make it into a great place. More and more people have made appointments with me to try to move out here. I even thought about it once or twice myself."

"Which had nothing to do with that certain, handsome-as-all-get-out resident millionaire who was single then, I'm sure." Cassie might have been tired, but she didn't let that dull her sense of humor. Or, maybe, she was trying to distract her sister.

Kristen snorted. "Hey, I'd like you to find me one woman in the entire zip code who wouldn't have changed addresses to get to James Callahan," she challenged.

Henry glanced over at Cassie. He didn't like being reminded that he didn't know many things about her, romantic life included. For all he knew, she could have been seeing someone.

Henry ground his teeth again at the thought of her being with another man.

He actively kept from gripping the steering wheel tighter.

"You got me there. James *is* a catch," Cassie admitted. "But I can also show you the *only* woman in the zip code who exists according to James."

There was a huff from the back seat.

Cassie smiled. She caught his eye and took pity on his utter lack of knowledge when it came to the personal intricacies of Riker County.

"That one woman is none other than our fearless leader."

"Suzy?"

Cassie nodded. "Her job is probably the only reason some crazed James fanatic hasn't tried to get in between the couple. Not that I think anyone could do that to start with." Her smile faded. Shadows covered her. The mood in the car shifted just like that. "It's his cabin we're going to. One that they've kept private. James even bought the land under his sister's boyfriend's name to keep people from prying. Unless they're local and friends with James and his family, I can't imagine anyone would even know it's there. I didn't until tonight."

Henry hoped that was true.

They drove in silence, following Kristen's GPS until it directed them to a dirt road on the very tip of the town. Rolling fields transitioned to thick woods of tall oaks and pines. The girls were just as alert as Henry felt maneuvering his car over the rough road. Both were leaning against their windows while he tried to survey their surroundings, looking for possible alternate escape routes or places where someone could hide a vehicle. He saw neither.

Two minutes or so into the drive, the road curved and the trees opened up. A small, true wooden cabin was nestled in a tight but clean clearing. No lights were on and no cars were parked in the small graveled parking area tucked next to the structure.

Henry left the car running and headlights on as he took the key Suzy had given him and went through the house. The cabin was less quaint on the inside but still cozy. It was also empty of any threats. The perfect place to let Cassie get some rest. Judging by the bags beneath her eyes and the slow gait she used between the passenger's side of the car and the living room, she truly needed it.

And apparently a hot bath.

"I've been rained on, twice, hidden in hotel bathrooms and back rooms of bars, not to mention walked through the aftermath of a shotgun blast." She crossed her arms over her chest. "If I don't get at least five minutes of sitting in a hot bath, I will probably throw a tantrum." She jutted her hip out and narrowed her eyes at Henry and Kristen. "Anything you need to do in there, you do it now."

In unison Kristen and Henry responded.

"Yes, ma'am."

The older Gates scurried off, brandishing her toothbrush while Henry put the bags she'd packed before going to the hospital in the bedroom.

Cassie sat on the edge of the bed and sighed. "Do you think Maggie is okay?"

The question didn't catch Henry off guard. He'd been waiting for it since they'd gotten the news. "I think she was taken for a reason." He straightened so he was opposite her. She looked up at him through her long eyelashes, worried and scared. It sent a shock through him at how close they were to each other.

And how much he wanted to be closer.

"Sometimes being taken for a reason rather than as an impulsive act can be a good thing."

"It might mean she's alive then," Cassie suggested. Henry nodded. "But if it's revenge these people are after, then the purpose she was taken for can't be good." Her shoulders sagged and her voice broke.

Henry lowered himself beside her and gently pulled her into his side. She didn't resist. The smell of her shampoo once again filled his senses.

In that moment all he wanted to do was to comfort her. "After the fire on the ranch, I was pulled from undercover work for a few months. I'd like to say it was for a lot of reasons, but mostly it was because I'd become difficult. All that work the task force had done, or I thought we'd done, and all I had to show for it was a few criminals behind bars and a dead partner. It didn't seem right."

Cassie kept her head at his shoulder but tilted her face up to show she was listening.

He continued. "I spiraled for a while. Drank some, then drank some more. Questioned life, my career, why I did what I did. Hit a low point and hit it hard. But, like I told you the night we met, I know what it's like to be the baby of the family. To be told what I needed rather than it being suggested. That's what my brother did. He drove eighteen hours straight out to my place, made me pack a bag and then made me drive the eighteen hours back."

He smiled. "In that time we talked about anything and everything. He didn't take no for an answer and pushed me to talk about stuff that I hadn't said to anyone. He made me face the pain of losing Calvin head-on. And then he made me face myself. You see, being undercover like we were wasn't just about lying. It was about making people believe." He fisted the hand not around Cassie. If she saw it, she didn't say anything. "I did some things I'm not proud of to keep my cover and that's just something I'm going to have to live with. But what had happened to Calvin was different. It changed me. So my brother asked me what I wanted out of life."

Cassie moved her head back to meet his gaze. Her eyes were shining but no tears stained her cheeks.

"I told him I wanted to protect people," he continued. "That's all I'd ever wanted to do. Help people and get justice for those who couldn't get it for themselves. And then he told me about a sheriff's department that had been in the news that wasn't too far from where I'd been in Tennessee." He felt a smile stretch over his lips. "The next week I applied. The week after that I drove in for an interview." He paused, wondering if he should keep going. But one look into those wide, clear eyes and he decided against it. This story wasn't about absolving him, it was about comforting her.

"I wanted and accepted the job at the sheriff's department because the part of me that has always wanted to do good, to keep people safe, to get the job *done*, saw that that's *exactly* what the Riker County Sheriff's Department did on a daily basis. They do good. They keep people safe. They *get the job done*. No matter what, or who, tries to stop them. You got that?"

A small but true smile lifted the corners of her lips. Cassie nodded.

"Now, I also firmly believe you meant business about taking that bath. So I'm going to leave you to that." He stood and grinned. "I've seen just how good a shot you are. I'm not about to tempt you to show me just how serious you are."

Henry went to the door, but Cassie spoke up.

Her smile was gone. "You gave me a fake name, said you didn't have a phone number, disappeared for seven months and then pretended not to know me when you showed up again." There was no heat in her words. No anger. Just statements. It was more effective than if she'd yelled. "I know we've said we'll talk about it later, but now that doesn't seem as important."

For the first time Henry saw Cassie ball her fist.

"I just wanted to say thank you for what you've done the past few days... But, honestly, I'm still mad. And I don't think there's anything you can say that will change that."

Kristen cleared her throat. Henry turned to see her outside the door, toothbrush in hand. She was frowning. Henry moved to let her by. She looked almost apologetic as she shut the door to the bedroom behind her.

## Chapter Eighteen

The bath was getting cold, the bubbles getting low. Kristen had laughed when she'd found the kid's bubble bath, but Cassie had been delighted. Sure, she liked soaking in the tub, but bubbles made it more fun. Or, at least, they had.

She leaned back in the shallow tub and moved the suds remaining around her like a blanket. Her body might have relaxed because of the heat, but her mind hadn't slowed.

From the attack to Maggie being taken.

From the fear of Henry being hurt to having to shoot a woman.

From Henry opening up and then to her letting him in.

Not to mention pregnancy hormones.

It was already a lot to take in without those making her emotions go haywire.

Part of Cassie wanted to cry in bed until she fell asleep.

The other wanted to scream and jump into a car in search for Maggie herself.

Another part, small but strong, asked for food. She'd eaten at the hospital, but that had been a few hours ago. It was now nearing one in the morning.

A soft knock rapped against the door. It startled her out of her thoughts.

"Come in."

The last person she thought would want to talk to her right now popped his head around the opened door. Despite her earlier flip from gratitude to anger at his speech, a thrill went through Cassie's naked body. She slid down into the water. Henry kept his eyes on hers, not looking down.

"I just wanted to check on you," he said, voice tight. "It's been a while. I was afraid you might have fallen asleep."

Cassie sighed. It moved the last of the bubbles across her chest.

"I thought I'd be more tired, I surely was earlier, but now all I am is worried, mad and hungry. It's like my mind and body won't sync up. How can I take what's going on seriously while all I can think of are dough-nuts?"

Henry held up his finger. "Maybe I can help with that."

He disappeared from the door frame. Cassie checked her bubbles again. Her stomach stuck out of the water an inch or so, but the rest of her was hidden. Unless he decided to come stand over her.

Henry being so near her naked again sent a shiver of longing through her.

Another thing she'd blame pregnancy hormones on.

She wanted to be mad that he'd lied, left and lied again. She wanted to put distance between them so she could sort her thoughts and figure out how to move on from them.

But was that even possible?

Could she get over Henry Ward?

Just the sight of him filling the doorway with his masculine frame was enough to send her body into another fit of yearning. His eyes so blue and so true lit up as he shook a bag in each of his hands. Cassie momentarily forgot to be mad.

"Before we left the hospital I grabbed a few things from the vending machine. Suzy pointed out these are some of your favorites?"

The man was holding a bag of chips and a pack of M&M's and he had never looked so sexy.

She could have cried.

"I swear you have just answered my prayers," she said, meaning it. Henry laughed and, keeping his eyes directly on hers, let her reach for the chips. She settled back into the water and opened the bag. Only after she smelled the chips did she feel heat crawl up her neck. "I bet I look like such a slob right now," she quipped.

Henry shook his head. "You look like a woman who's had a hard day." It was a smart thing to say. "Which you have. If there was a hot tub, I might be in there right now with these."

He shook the candy bag she'd left him and started for the door. Cassie didn't like the thought of him leaving. It made her angry at herself. Then angry at him. Then angry at herself for being angry.

"Wait," she called. "If you want, you can stay in here for a little bit." The blush already burning her cheeks became hotter. Still she pushed through it. "I wouldn't mind the company."

Henry didn't argue. He shut the door and sat on the floor, back against it. For a minute they both ate their snacks in silence. It was enough time to sort her thoughts out. She finished off the bag of chips and rested it against her floating belly. With a sigh that had been one of many through the last seven months, Cassie finally got to the heart of what was bothering her.

All while sitting in the bathtub.

"Okay, so I guess it was my fault."

Henry's eyes found hers and held. His eyebrow arched high. "What was your fault?"

"I was naive," she started after a long exhale. She idly began to move a cluster of bubbles next to her belly with one of her hands. It weirdly helped her nerves. "See, my parents have been with each other since they were fifteen. During their life together they've had six kids. Of those six, four have spouses they're mad about. I mean, over the moon, would do anything for, and two even have those tacky, matching tattoos. Being around them, you can just feel it, too. Like they've found their purpose in life within each other. Just like how our parents are. So, it sounds silly, but all I've known of relationships is true and unending love."

She gave him a wry smile, trying to let him know that she realized what she said probably sounded cheesy. As usual, his expression was guarded. She could no more tell if he thought she was crazy than if he was even listening to her at all. But what she knew of the man, she was sure he was. "Now, I've dated and been with men before. But there was never a connection. Never anything that was like what my family had talked about feeling. That is until the night I met you."

The courage that had filled her chest the moment before started to wane. She averted her gaze but only for a moment. "That night I felt what I thought was a connection with you. A spark. That's why I came to your room, that's why I gave you my number and that's why I shared your bed. I broke character for the first time in my life because I thought I was following some kind of invisible road to what had made my family happy for decades. I didn't care that I had only known you for a few hours. It didn't matter."

A lump formed in her throat. Tears welled up behind her eyes. Cassie refused to stop for either. "But I…I was naive. And so I waited for a call, a text. Heck, I would have been happy with a friend request. But nothing came. That's when I realized that my family wasn't average. What they had was special and rare and beautiful."

The tears that had threatened now fell down her cheeks. "And that made me proud of them, of where I come from. But…but then I felt like a little girl who'd just been told Santa didn't exist. That love was more complicated than some magical connection. And then… then I found out I was pregnant and the most extraordinary thing happened. The heart I'd just been worried would never find someone to love was stolen by someone I hadn't even met yet." She touched her stomach, feeling the love for her child radiate throughout her. She smiled through her tears. "During the next few months I realized that, while my life had taken a different, maybe unconventional, path compared to my parents' and siblings', it didn't mean it wasn't special in its own right."

Henry's brows knitted together, his jaw hardened. "Cassie, I—"

She shook her head. She wasn't to the point yet. The real reason she realized she was so angry. "I also took that time to come to terms with the fact that I'd probably never see you again. I even got used to the idea. Then, all of a sudden, there you were. Walking into that diner wearing a shiny deputy's badge. And just like that I was back standing at that pool table, laughing at your jokes."

Henry got to his feet and started to close the gap between them. Cassie couldn't read his expression. She didn't care. She had to say her piece. She had to let them both know what she was feeling because, soon, there would be three of them.

"After everything that had happened, everything that was going haywire around us, and there you were. Smiling at me over that pool table with those baby blues. I guess I knew then I couldn't deny it anymore."

Henry got to his knees on the tile next to the tub. If he wanted, he could see all of her by just glancing down. But she knew he wouldn't. He wasn't that kind of guy. He didn't take without asking. Or, well, maybe he did.

Henry was so close she couldn't help reaching out. He let her trace the sharp line of his jaw as she continued.

"While my son might have taken all my heart, there was still something inside me that just wouldn't let go of you."

A breath barely stretched between the end of her admission and the beginning of their kiss. Henry moved over the lip of the tub so Cassie didn't have to move an inch. Not that she could. She hadn't been fishing for affection from the man. She'd just wanted him to know what she felt. With the madness of everything that had happened, it had been nice to say something certain.

Now what was certain was the hardness of his lips against hers. The prickle of his facial hair against her fingers. Her mouth parting so his tongue could delve deeper.

The way one kiss could somehow touch every fiber of her being.

Henry moved his hands to either side of her face and softened the kiss until he broke it. He was smiling.

"Cassie Gates, I want to show you something."

He released her, to Cassie's utter surprise, and pulled out his wallet. She couldn't stop her eyebrow from shooting straight up toward her hairline. He opened the worn leather and pulled something out from behind the plastic protector that held his license. It was a piece of paper. A small piece, ripped from the corner of a hotel notepad.

Cassie knew this because she'd been the one to do it.

Henry held the paper up. "The day you gave this to me, I interviewed for a job and was offered that same job on the spot. I accepted it and went straight home, resigned, and had to start tying up loose ends. I gave you a false last name on the off chance you tried to track me down before I could finish because I didn't want you to get tangled up in my old life. I had decided that after I was finished, and got a new number and officially was done with that life, I would call you."

His smile wavered. Cassie hung on his every word.

"But then my boss pulled me in for one last job that he said needed Gage Coulson. He told me it would be quick. It wasn't. I finished it up a month ago." With one hand he reached out and moved a wayward strand of her hair behind her ear. Then he was looking at her like she'd never been looked at before. "I should have still called or done something or *said* something when

I did finally see you. But, Cassie Gates, I was a damn idiot." That smile found its footing again. "You're the most beautiful woman I've ever seen, and even though I'm an idiot, I kept this piece of paper with your number on it because I'd always hoped I'd see you again. If only to kiss you at least one more time."

Cassie dropped her gaze to her handwriting across the paper. He'd really kept it. For seven months. He'd kept it in his wallet.

"I know you said there isn't anything I could say to make you not be angry with me, and that's fine," he continued, voice lowering. "I just was tired of being quiet about something I should have already said."

Henry's face, for once, wasn't closed. The walls that he'd been guarding himself with were all gone. He'd opened himself up to her, finally, and now was waiting for her to set the new tone for them. His baby blues searched her face, his lips slunk downward and just when he looked like his was about to move away, Cassie decided what that tone would be for them.

"So," she started, trying to keep her expression neutral. "After seven months of waiting, you decided the best time to kiss me was when I was naked, sitting in a cold tub, surrounded by strawberry-scented bubbles, *completely* hormonal, and with an empty bag of chips sitting on my swollen belly? I have to say, Deputy Ward, I know we might have done this relationship a bit backward, but in the future I wouldn't mind some romance in my life."

Henry's smile resurfaced and then turned into a grin. "Yes, ma'am."

## Chapter Nineteen

The rain was a fine mist outside, cooling the ground but not hurting the view. Henry was like a sullen child, pouting as he stared out the window. He'd been in the same state for almost twenty minutes, just watching the wooded area surrounding the cabin. It gave Cassie the time to watch him in turn.

Broad shoulders nearly blocked the window's width, filling out his flannel button-up to the point of where it was tight across his biceps. Whatever he had been doing in the last several months, she would bet lifting weights had been a part of his routine. Just as wearing those jeans must also have been on his docket. You just didn't get that shade of faded denim store-bought. That was true wear and tear. It was amazing it even kept that tush of his in.

Cassie's gaze had traveled over that very tush and down across his thighs and calves. She knew them just as intimately as the rest of the man. Taut, muscled and hard from an active lifestyle.

In fact, she didn't know if there was a spot on the man that was soft.

She traced his profile back to the line of his jaw where stubble had sprouted. Then her eyes went to the last feature of the man she hadn't admired yet in detail.

There *was* a softness to his lips. After they had shared their feelings in the bathroom, they'd taken to the couch in the living room. There they'd touched on almost every topic under the sun. There he'd given her more than a fair share of gentle, sweet kisses. Ones that filled her with hope, comfort and had eventually made her feel safe enough to fall asleep.

Now, an hour or two after she'd woken, he had his eyes outside and his mind somewhere else. She wished she could make him feel better. Just like she wished she could help the men and women of the department who, according to him, hadn't had any luck in finding Maggie or the rest of the culprits.

Cassie kept her sigh close to her chest and let her eyes dance across the man who could put fire in her body just by standing still.

The same man who apparently wasn't as oblivious as she'd thought.

"You stare at me much longer and I might just have to charge you for it."

A muscle in Henry's jaw twitched, trying to keep in a smirk, no doubt.

Cassie felt heat start to crawl up her neck. That had less to do with being caught admiring the man's body and more to do with how hers had reacted to the memory of what it had felt like against hers. South of her waistline was already heated.

And was already wanting more.

There he was again, a fire starter wearing denim so well it was almost criminal.

"I was just wondering how long you were going to sulk," she said, keeping her tone light. "You're acting like you were the last boy to be picked for kickball, and you know that's just not the case."

Another small twitch in his jaw let her know she'd hit on some of his humor. It was brief. Even if they'd made headway about the two of them, there was still a county of hurting outside the cabin's walls.

"I spent months trying to get away from my old job, an old life, and still, after a week here, I bring trouble hot on my heels." He moved over so she could take up position at his side. The sky was nearly crystal blue. If storms were coming, they were being slow about it.

"Trouble follows this job." Cassie touched his shoulder to underline the point. "It might have followed you, but it also followed Caleb and Suzy and a whole bunch of people. That's just the way of the job. You do enough good and you're bound to reap some of the bad you helped stop."

"But Calvin is my bad. And if he really did orchestrate the attacks yesterday…"

Cassie saw his frown. She felt it in her bones. Just as

she saw the guilt weighing down his body. She felt it, too. She wanted to stop both. Or, at least, lessen them.

"No one is going to blame you for Calvin. No matter what he does, he did it. Not you. Plain and simple."

Henry looked down his nose at her, eyes the color of any woman's favorite pair of blue jeans. Which might just be the ones he was wearing, Cassie decided.

"You know you Riker County people have a habit of sounding like fortune cookies. First the 'some people suck' thing and now 'trouble follows the job'?"

Cassie made a face as he smirked.

"I mean no disrespect. Just saying you all might need to look into designing those inspirational office posters. You know, the ones with cats hanging from things and nice words over pictures of sunsets. Might be a good source of extra income for the department."

Cassie couldn't help snorting at that.

It earned a small smile from the man.

Again, that didn't last long, either. He didn't have to say a word. Cassie knew he was still being eaten up from the inside. Memories of his former partner, worries of his new department and the giant unknown connecting both.

"Here, I know what might help." Cassie reached out and took the man's hand. Despite his inner turmoil he wrapped his fingers around hers, protectively. They were warm and strong.

Cassie directed the man through the living room to the kitchen and out its back door. The temperature had indeed cooled, but once the mist left over by the rain was completely gone, the sticky heat would make up for the change. Until then she marched them through the yard and right into the trees.

"We shouldn't be out here," Henry said, head already on a swivel. He didn't get out of her pull, but she heard the distinct sound of him freeing his gun from its holster.

"No one knows where this place is. We've been here for hours. If Calvin or Michael or anyone else manages to show up, then color me impressed." She gave him a little tug as he started to resist when she said Calvin's name. "Plus, isn't that a gun in your hand? If anyone comes out at us, shoot 'em!"

She heard him chuckle but kept on forward.

"You know, since I started, everyone keeps telling me how sweet and calm you are, but sometimes I think they don't really know you," he said matter-of-factly. "Instead of honey, you're more like hot sauce. But the kind they try to hide in one of those bottles with the pretty wrappers."

Cassie dropped his hand as they moved through the trees, trying to keep herself balanced. The ground was filled with thick, twisting roots. The last thing she wanted to do was to face-plant in front of the deputy.

The deputy who seemed to think she was a bottle of hot sauce in a pretty wrapper.

"You don't think I'm sweet?" Cassie asked with mock offense. She placed her hand on a tree, trying to navigate around a few of its gnarled roots. It didn't work. One foot slipped off. It was enough to tip her entire balance off. Her stomach probably didn't help matters. All she had time to do was yelp.

One strong, solid arm looped around her waist. Henry stopped her fall by pulling her to him. Suddenly she could feel his warmth through the back of her shirt, feel his heartbeat thump between them. Cassie tried to laugh off her embarrassment and the heat that it brought to her body.

But she couldn't bring herself to make a sound.

Henry's hold on her didn't loosen. He didn't step back. He didn't try to turn her around. Cassie placed her hand on his arm. The fabric of his flannel was impossibly thick.

"You okay?" he asked.

Henry's voice had filled with grit, low and heady, near her ear. His breath skated across her skin. It didn't just stir feelings within her, it ignited them. Fire starter in denim, indeed. Cassie closed her eyes. Now wasn't the time.

"Cassie."

It wasn't a question. It felt more like a declaration.

Henry used the arm at her waist to slowly turn Cassie around. One look up at those soft lips and hers parted in anticipation. The deputy replaced his gun in his holster and then, slowly, closed what little distance there had been between them.

The woods around them quieted.

All there was were two people, each breathing heavy and searching for something the other might just have. Past and future be damned, Cassie wanted the man who'd given her her son right then and there.

Closing her eyes, she tilted her head up, anticipation tightening her entire body. All the man had to do was meet her halfway.

HENRY'S PULSE WAS RACING. His body winding up, ready for the woman he still held by the hip. Sure, they'd kissed the night before, but this was different. This feeling was almost carnal. This feeling was need.

One his body decided to give in to.

Her lips were soft, warm and inviting as Henry pressed against them. He laced his fingers into her hair, holding her fast. A moan escaped between them.

It unleashed the reservations inside Henry.

Moving carefully but pointedly, he pushed Cassie backward until she was against the bark of the closest tree. He braced one hand against that very bark. His tongue swept past her teeth and met hers, keeping the kiss. And then deepening it. Familiar territory.

But that didn't mean he was about to stop exploring.

He slipped his hand from her hair back to her hip, meaning to pull her even more against him. To show her that his attraction to her hadn't lessened in their time apart. His jeans were already growing tight at the zipper with how much he wanted the woman.

However, she was two steps ahead.

Her hands found his backside faster than a canine unit could find drugs in a dealer's den. She cupped his cheeks hard, using the force to try to pull *him* closer. It was enough of a surprise that Henry couldn't help the laugh that bubbled up in his throat.

Cassie broke their kiss, eyes hooded and lips dark, but kept her hands firmly in their respective places.

"What?" she asked, breathless.

"Never had a woman manhandle me like this before."

Not even an ounce of embarrassment passed over her expression. Instead her eyebrow rose high. "Wearing jeans like this and you're surprised I'm admiring your *assets*? I never took you for the modest type, Deputy Ward. I surely never took you for a fool." She took the smallest of moments to straighten her shoulders and jut out her chin, resolute. "Plus, pregnancy hormones are a very real thing."

Another laugh leaped from his chest. It was loud, genuine and seemed to please the woman. A beautiful smile pulled up the corners of a set of perfect, sexy, plump lips.

It was those lips he caught again in a quick kiss.

"See?" he said, pulling away to speak. "Hot. Sauce."

The sound of a branch splitting somewhere behind them changed the mood in an instant. Cassie let go of him as Henry pivoted around, careful to keep her behind him, gun already being pulled out and up.

Kristen's hands flew up in surrender.

"Well, this is awkward," Kristen hurriedly said.

Cassie let out a sigh.

"What are you doing out here?" she asked her sister, heavy with the annoyance in her voice.

Henry put his gun back in its holster and angled his body so Cassie could get a better view of her older sister. The woman looked between them with a knowing expression.

"I would ask what *you* two are doing out here, but I think that's apparent," she shot back. "As for me, I heard you two sneak out and got worried. We *are* supposed to be keeping a low profile, right?"

The unmistakable thuds of car doors shutting sounded behind them, back at the cabin. Henry pulled that gun right back out. No one had called Cassie's phone. No one was supposed to show up.

And even if Suzy Simmons or James Callahan had wanted to, they shouldn't have brought so many people.

Before Henry could move Cassie to the other side of the tree they'd been against, he had counted at least six car doors shutting.

"Calvin?" she whispered.

Henry didn't respond. The sound of glass shattering seemed to be answer enough that whoever the guests were, they weren't friendly.

"We need to go," he said, already moving backward. He took Cassie's hand as Kristen hurried to their side. "Try to be quiet," he warned. His heart thrummed in his ears. One man he could take on. Two or three, maybe, depending on the situation. But five or six?

If he lost, Cassie and Kristen would be targeted next.

No, he would try to get them to safety first and then—

"Hey! I see something!"

And just like that, the plan changed.

Henry cursed and spun on his heel, dropping Cassie's hand.

"Go," he instructed over his shoulder. "I'll hold them off."

Cassie stopped, shaking her head. "I'm not leaving you!"

"I'll be right behind you," he lied. "I just need to scare them off to give you some time."

Cassie's face contorted into an emotion he couldn't place. He didn't have time.

"Kristen, take her," he ordered, voice going hard. Two figures in the distance were coming through the trees.

"Come on, Cassie." Cassie must have resisted. Kristen's voice had also taken on an edge. "Think of your son."

Henry didn't take his eyes off the men coming through the trees at them, but he was keenly aware of the sounds behind him.

The sound of Cassie running away.

## Chapter Twenty

One man wore all black. The other also wore a ski mask. Both had guns. Neither was prepared for Henry.

Wanting to give the girls more time to escape, he checked his gun and ran straight toward the men. It apparently wasn't what they wanted.

The man wearing the mask hesitated, misstepped and toppled over with a yell. His friend in all black was more graceful in his surprise. His eyes widened, but his gun remained steady. He sent off two shots just as Henry took aim and fired his.

Bark next to Henry's head splintered and a quick burn of pain lit up the side of his leg, but all of his focus was on the man. Henry's bullet hit his stomach and down he went.

Now it was time to make sure his mask-wearing friend stayed down.

He closed one eye, pictured where he wanted to hit, and pulled the trigger.

Ski Mask gave another yell. This time in pain.

Henry was upon him in seconds, picking up his gun.

The man in black was unconscious, but Henry wasn't going to take any chances. He put the new gun in the back of his jeans and hurried to the fallen pistol. Ski Mask was angry. He cradled his shoulder but stayed on the ground.

"You son of a—"

A gunshot echoed through the trees. Henry ducked behind the one closest to him. He needed to reevaluate his strategy. Anyone and everyone at the cabin or in the surrounding woods would have heard the shots clear as day. The advancing shooter might be by himself now, but his numbers could quickly multiply.

Henry took a quick breath, adrenaline pumping hard throughout his system. He ducked low and swung around the tree. The gunman wasn't anyone he recognized, but he was admittedly a better shot than those who had preceded him.

The bullet tore through Henry's shirt, hot pain pushing into his skin. It threw off his trigger hand and aim. He shot close enough to make the man take temporary cover but not close enough to do any damage.

"You hit him," yelled the man in the mask.

Henry cursed something awful, wishing he'd rendered Ski Mask unconscious. His words alone rallied the man in the distance. He sent off another shot around the tree. Henry ducked to the side, barely clearing it.

He needed a better position to hold or else he'd be in real trouble sooner rather than later.

His arm burned, angry at being used after taking

a bullet, as he pulled up his weapon, ready to stop the third unknown man.

He didn't get the chance.

Another gunshot filled the air. The man who had shot him made no noise as a bullet went through his head. Henry stalled in his current action, stunned.

Calvin stood farther behind the now dead man.

He was aiming at Henry but shouted an order to the world around them.

"No one take a shot at Henry Ward or I will kill them, too. Understood?"

Henry had thought his situation was already one-sided. Sure, he'd taken down two men, but he'd assumed there were more.

He'd assumed correctly.

Yells of confirmation sounded off in the distance, near the cabin. However, a few came from the one place he didn't need them to be.

Behind him.

"You're thinking about trying to shoot as many of us as you can," Calvin called from his spot several yards away. "But I promise you that I came prepared."

A woman's scream made Henry's insides go cold. He spun around, not caring that his back was to Calvin. Paula walked out from behind a cluster of trees smiling. At the end of her shotgun was Kristen.

Her eyes were wide, terrified.

"First you're holed up in a hotel with a pregnant woman and now you're traipsing through the woods with this one?" Paula shook her head. "And here I was hoping I'd get a chance to say the first thank-you for my new scar." She motioned to her shoulder. It was bandaged. Henry shared a glance with Kristen. She gave nothing away.

"Well, now that we have what we need, I think it's time we get started," Calvin said.

Henry turned to watch Calvin's smirk dissolve. "Like you said, only children play games. And now it's time to be an adult."

Henry's mind raced, filling with questions and fears and plans that might save them.

However, above the whirl of noise, there was one question that stayed loudest.

Where was Cassie?

"STOP *BITING* ME!"

Michael managed to free his hand, but Cassie was more than ready to try again. Hands tied behind her back or not, she had enough adrenaline and rage pumping through her that she was positive she could do some damage.

"Oh, I'm sorry, am I causing *you* discomfort?" she yelled. The sound bounced off the wall around them. Without the blindfold over her eyes she had to squint against the sunlight filtering through the closest window. "Considering you're the one who *kidnapped* me, *blindfolded and gagged* me, and now *have tied me to a chair*, that's truly rich."

Cassie struggled against the rope around her wrists. They weren't that tight. If she could slip out of them, maybe she'd have a fighting chance.

Michael took off his suit jacket. Wherever they were, along with not having any furniture, the place didn't seem to have air-conditioning, either.

"I had to get you out of there as fast and as quietly as I could," he said. "I didn't think you'd just believe that I was trying to save you."

Cassie felt her eyebrow rise. She snorted. "Trying to save me?"

Michael rolled his eyes and looked at the half-moon mark she'd just left on his hand. He sighed. "Despite what you may think of me, I'm not some cold-hearted thug. I was paid to find Henry Ward and get him to meet with Calvin. I knew he was looking for revenge, but I didn't know how far he would take it. He saw you drag Henry into the house to protect him yesterday. He decided he wanted to use you against the deputy. I tried to warn you, but that had the opposite effect, apparently."

Cassie tilted her head to the side, confused.

"Why?" she asked. "Why do you care about me? We don't even know each other."

Michael looked at her belly. His expression actually softened. "My wife's pregnant."

Cassie knew she could be naive sometimes, too kind at others. But in that moment, with those three words, she believed the man standing in front of her. Still, that didn't mean she had to be happy about it.

"Why didn't you grab my sister, too? Why not help Henry?" Fear gripped her chest. "What happened to them? Do you know where they are? Where are we? What happens now?"

Michael shook his head. "Paula was too close to grab you both. One look at you and I'm pretty sure she would have forgotten who her boss was and repaid you for shooting her. She doesn't hold that anger for your sister. Hell, unless they say something, I don't think they'll make the connection that you two are related. I was the only person who did my homework. That was only my job."

The pit of Cassie's stomach fell to the floor. "So Kristen is with Paula and Calvin? Is Henry, too?"

An emotion crossed Michael's face. She couldn't tell what it was. Regardless, it scared her.

"Yeah, Calvin and his band of merry men took them both, and as far as I know they're still alive. But…" He glanced at the window. "When I was leaving with you, he spotted my car. I knew if I tried to run he'd send someone after us. So I came back to where we've been hiding out. Luckily he was preoccupied or else he might have noticed I waited until they were out of sight before bringing you in."

Cassie didn't understand. "So you kidnapped me to keep me from getting kidnapped, or worse, but then brought me to the place I was originally going to be taken to if I *had* been kidnapped?"

Michael ran his hand through his red hair, frustration evident. "Nobody's perfect, Miss Gates."

HENRY HIT THE floor hard. Blood ran down his arm and shirt, hitting the wood next to him. Dust kicked up against his face. He groaned.

"Fun fact, those are your cuffs." Calvin laughed. "The ones, I'd like to point out, that I took off you probably a few feet from here. Give or take."

Henry rolled onto his side and then his back. He recognized the room. Though the last time he'd been in it he had been staring at the face of a beautiful woman. Now he was staring at the face of a sick man.

He only hoped that wherever Cassie had hidden, she was safe.

"Where did you take Kristen?" he asked, barely able to form words around his anger. She'd been put in the same car as him and used as a way to keep Henry from fighting. Once they'd entered the old neighborhood of Westbridge and parked outside the same house he and Cassie had taken refuge in the day before, Paula had taken Kristen in a different direction. Henry had bucked around then and earned quite the proficient beating from one of the seemingly countless lackeys Calvin had roped in. He'd also earned the being handcuffed at his back. "What are you going to do with her?"

Calvin leaned against the wall. He nodded for the man who had brought Henry in to leave. He didn't speak until the door closed in the next room over.

"She's fine for now." He was wearing the same grin he'd had on since he'd ordered Henry into the car. "But you know the drill. You do anything crazy and I go get her and make sure she's *not* fine."

Henry sat up, using the wall closest to him for support. The bullet had gone through his arm, but it didn't detract from the pain. Not that he had room to complain. He needed to find a way to get to Kristen so they could escape. Cassie wouldn't forgive him otherwise. And neither would he forgive himself if anything happened to her. Especially at Calvin's hands.

"I don't understand," he decided on proclaiming. He needed to buy time to gather back some of his strength. What better way than to try to get some answers? "I saw you get shot in that barn and now you're back terrorizing some small Alabama town with a whole crew of criminals? Why?"

Calvin laughed again. This time Henry heard the bitterness in it.

"You know, the first time we met I thought we had the potential to be a great duo. Heck, I *knew* it. When we were busting up fights on calls, chasing down idiots who thought they could get away, or just trying to find the lie some hapless druggie would try to pass off on us, we just had the right groove going. And then *bam!* we started going undercover." He clapped his hands together. "What do you know? We were just as good at being bad guys as we were at being good guys!"

"It was an act," Henry said defensively, shame and anger coursing through him. "It was a job!"

Calvin's face contorted. He slammed his fist against the wall. The window next to him shook.

"It was a goal," he yelled. "One that I realized we could achieve!" He spread his hands out wide. "Instead of spending every day watching as men and women with a whole lot less intelligence than us prosper from doing *a whole lot less* than we did, I saw an end-game. I didn't need to *pretend* I wanted it, and that only made it easier to get."

Henry felt like he was going to be sick. How had he missed the change in Calvin?

How had he not known?

"So, what? You're just going to be a crime show's cliché?" Henry asked. "A cop who went undercover and then blurred the line between right and wrong?"

Calvin laughed with no smile. His mood swings were throwing off Henry's ever-changing opinion of the man. Maybe he wasn't stable anymore. Maybe he was so far gone that trying to make sense of him was impossible.

"See, Henry, that's you to a tee," he said. "You sit there and think a thousand thoughts but won't say what you *really* think until you're pushed. That's what made you so great at going undercover. You could sit in silence trying to figure out your next move and everyone just thought it was a part of some dumb criminal. Right now I bet you're trying to figure out why I am the way I am. What happened? What signs did *you* miss when it came to my descent into—" he motioned to himself with a wave of his hands "—whatever it is I am now?"

Calvin crossed the room and stopped just short of Henry's boots. He bent over and jabbed his finger in the air, level with his eyes.

"I want you to listen, and I want you to listen good," he continued venomously. "This had nothing to do with what you did and didn't do. This is about me. See, there was never any blurring of lines. Never just one assignment that sent me over the edge. Henry, there was never even an edge to begin with. Do you want to know why?"

Henry kept his mouth shut. His fists were balled against the floor. The blood from his gunshot turned cold against his skin.

Calvin's face was red. He spit as he spoke. "I was *always* on the ground knowing exactly what it was that I wanted out of life. I wanted to be bad. It just took me a while to figure it out."

"Then why come here? Why come after me? You could have stayed off the radar. No one suspected you made it out of that barn. Definitely not me."

Calvin answered him with another question. "Do you remember why Arnold earned law enforcement's attention in the first place?"

Henry knew this answer. "He gained a lot of power really quickly."

Calvin snapped his fingers together. "Exactly! And remember how he did that?" This time he wasn't looking for an answer. "Arnold Richland inspired loyalty among almost everyone who worked for him through mass example. He promised power and money and delivered on both so quickly that, yeah, it brought him to our attention, but it also got him a small army. One that is majorly still out there."

Henry ground his teeth. "No thanks to you, I assume."

Calvin smirked again. "I wondered if you'd figure out it was me who tipped the Richlands off that night. Though, admittedly, I'd been aligned with them for a few months by that point. It took a *lot* of convincing to keep Arnold from killing you."

Henry was seeing red.

"Then why give me a show of you being killed if you were just going to leave me in the barn to die?" he yelled.

Calvin was unperturbed by the change in volume.

"Arnold told me about the beginnings of his rise to power one night," he continued. "Apparently a few of his first followers questioned just how far he was willing to go to see their group succeed. Especially when it came to his little brother, Reggie. Do you remember him?"

Henry didn't answer, but Calvin did. He continued, once again unperturbed by his audience's anger. "He was a preacher. Nice, humble and the direct opposite of what Arnold wanted to be. The yin to his yang. That's how he knew what needed to be done. He had to kill Reggie to prove himself."

Henry could have been sick.

"Is that what I am?" he asked. "I'm your opposite so you have to kill me to make some kind of twisted point?"

Calvin simply nodded. "When you were trapped in that burning building, I thought, 'Well, hey, that's easy.' But then I found out you were alive. And not only that, but you were trying to make a new home for yourself in Alabama." He shrugged. "What better place to start my own rise to power? There was definitely no short supply of anger and resentment when it came to the sheriff's department. It made it almost too easy to find recruits. All I had to do was promise them revenge. Heck, I even sweetened the pot by convincing them that if they waited, played the parts I gave them, I'd give them a plan that ensured not only revenge but suffering, too."

"It didn't work," Henry pointed out. "Not on the scale I'm sure you promised, at least."

Calvin shrugged, the very picture of indifference. "What I promised them was the chance to get what they wanted. If they failed in following through, that's on them. All they wanted from me was the tools to attempt it. Not my fault that the idiot Darrel decided to take out his rage on the sheriff before it was time. Some minds are too small to see the big picture."

"And what now? Waiting for another storm?"

Calvin shook his head. "My demonstration has already gained me interest. Now your death will gain me loyalty."

Henry's muscles started to tense. His mind hadn't stopped whirling. He thought of Cassie, of his son, of Kristen, Maggie, Matt, Caleb and Alyssa. He thought of everyone else he'd met since coming to Riker County. He thought of Hawk, a man he'd fought beside, and Suzy, a woman who had earned his burden by proximity alone. He thought of Billy and his family. He even thought of Gary, the man at the bar who had been too drunk to see just how amazing the blonde asking him to buy her a drink was.

But most of all, he thought of Calvin Fitzgerald.

A man who had been a part of his life for years.

He had been hilarious, smart, ridiculous, kind when it counted, thoughtful when it was called for, and an absolute lightweight when it came to tequila.

He'd been the best friend Henry had ever had.

And as far as Henry was concerned, Calvin Fitzgerald had never come out of that barn in Tennessee.

Instead of feeling another wave of mourning that had knocked him on his ass after the fire, Henry felt something else spreading throughout him.

"You say I never really knew you, and that may be true," he breathed.

It wasn't a statement. It wasn't a speech. It didn't even feel like words. He was talking, but everything was shifting in each sound. Slowly, Henry tucked his legs and stood. The Calvin in front of him, a man built on ego and a broken moral compass, gave him the room to do it.

He hadn't realized it yet.

For all his skill and experience, Calvin Fitzgerald hadn't seen the signs.

He didn't know he'd already lost.

"Memory Lane is a two-way street," Henry said. All pain and anger left him. All that was left was the promise of justice right around the corner. It was just waiting for him to take it. "I may not know you, but you *do* know me."

This time it was Henry that smiled.

"So, I ask you, *partner*, what would Henry Ward normally do in *this* situation?"

A second of silence moved between them.

Then Calvin's face fell. His glee and ego with it. Lines of worry stretched across his expression and his eyes widened to make room for fear.

Still, he answered, "He'd fight like hell."

Henry rolled his shoulders back. "I guess you really do know me."

Then he charged.

## Chapter Twenty-One

Cassie swatted Michael away.

He rolled his eyes.

"I'm trying to help you, woman," he whispered. "Let me go in first."

They were standing at the back end of a decrepit deck, careful to keep out of sight of the car sitting out front. Michael had a snazzy revolver in his hand, while Cassie had pregnancy hormones. They weren't being nice, either. Since Michael had made her promise not to try to escape or, worse, try to take on Calvin by herself, he'd untied her and given her two options.

She could wait in the house, hiding until Calvin and his goons left and then sneak out, or he could sneak her into his car and make up an excuse to leave.

Then Cassie had given him two choices.

He could either sit by like a coward while potentially two women and a good, good man were killed, or he could set an example for his future child by helping to save the father of *her* future child.

He had said some not-so-good words and now they

were about to sneak into a house where he'd seen Kristen taken. So, basically, he'd made the only right choice.

"Cassie," he warned when she still wouldn't retreat behind him. "They think I'm on their team, remember?"

She took a deep breath, annoyed, but nodded. He put his gun behind his back and stood tall. Cassie followed him and then ducked to the side as he knocked on the door. Footfalls stirred inside. Cassie didn't have time to evaluate just how terrified she should be. She put her hand on her stomach. All she knew was that no one was going to take any part of her son's family away from him.

The door opened, but she couldn't see the person on the other side. Judging by Michael's lack of pulling his gun, she assumed they knew each other. Then she heard her.

"Hey, Paula, how's the arm?"

The woman snorted. "Nothing a dead pregnant chick wouldn't fix."

Cassie's blood went cold.

Michael kept a straight face.

"Sounds like you have some issues to work out," he said with a good dose of annoyance. "Until then, Calvin told me to come talk to the blond woman. See if I could find anything out from her."

Paula huffed. "Good luck. I already tried to beat some sense into her, but she kept her mouth shut."

Cassie's rage nearly blinded her.

Michael took a small step forward.

"I have a way with words," he said.

Paula made a noise that Cassie was ready to bet was accompanied by her rolling her eyes.

"Whatever."

She must have turned away. In a move that was truly the epitome of graceful, he leaped forward through the doorway. Cassie didn't wait on the sidelines any longer. She sprang in behind him, ready to do some damage, but came up short.

Michael had Paula in a headlock, one hand over her mouth. Cassie hurried and closed the door behind them, hoping no one outside had heard the scuffle. The dark-haired woman raged against the man, fighting him and unconsciousness. She kicked back and flailed until her heel came up right where the sun didn't shine.

Michael held in his groan of pain and his hold on her drooped. Cassie wasn't having any of it. She lunged forward and punched the spot where she'd shot the woman the day before.

That did the trick.

She cried out around Michael's hand but had lost some of her fight. It was enough to let the man get the upper hand. Finally, Paula went limp.

Michael was less graceful about dropping her unconscious body to the floor.

"I am not a fan of that woman," he said, out of breath.

Cassie would have agreed, but movement in the corner of the room caught her attention.

It was Kristen, tied up to a chair, but alive.

Cassie could have cried as she hurried to her older sister's side. She ripped the duct tape off her mouth.

"Are you okay?" Cassie asked, restraining her emotions to a low voice.

"Is there anyone else in the house?" Michael asked at her shoulder.

Kristen had a bruise across her face and blood on her cheek. There were also signs of a black eye. But she answered quickly with a voice that didn't waver.

"That horrible woman was the only one I ever saw in here. Everyone else went back out to the car or drove off." She turned her gaze to Cassie. "Maggie is in the next room."

Michael nodded and started for the door.

"Let Cassie go instead," Kristen advised hurriedly. "Maggie already roughed up two men. The only reason they didn't kill her was that Calvin stepped in." Her eyes moved back to Cassie's. They glassed over. "They separated me and Henry. I don't know where he is, but he tried really hard to save me."

Cassie gave her sister a quick kiss on the cheek.

"It's okay. We're going to save him, too," she said, resolute. "Michael, untie her, please. I'll get Maggie."

Bless him, he did just that.

HENRY SENT CALVIN crashing through the window. The force of the righteousness he felt in his chest, plus the running start and mass of muscle he had on him, helped break the glass against his old partner's back.

Then they were airborne.

Then the ground met them with a vengeance.

Calvin's breath made a noise as it left his body from the impact. Henry's body rag-dolled off him. Glass and pain were shared between them.

But then it was time to finish what Henry had started.

He rolled over onto his knees, grinding glass against the grass and dirt beneath him. Calvin might have been surprised and in pain, but if there was one thing they had established, it was that he *did* know Henry.

Which meant he knew he had to recover fast or else he'd lose.

He rolled onto his side, still wheezing. He was going to go for the gun at his back. The same one that must have hurt like hell to land on.

Henry leaned back to his ankle. His hands might have still been cuffed, but he could reach the one thing he knew Calvin hadn't taken from him. By the time Calvin was struggling to stand and pull his gun, Henry already had the knife in his hands and was on his feet.

Again he charged forward. He pushed his shoulder into the man and then spun around. Calvin saw it a second too late. The knife stuck into the side of his stomach. His pain and fear made him drop his gun. Henry kicked it to the side.

Calvin let out a wild sound that Henry couldn't quite define. The man swung his famous knock-out hit, but this time Henry knew it was coming. He dodged the hit but kept close.

Using a move he'd been on the receiving end of the night before, Henry executed one of the top five favorite techniques of his career.

He head-butted Calvin so hard that he heard the man's nose break.

It was the final blow.

Calvin fell backward again.

This time he didn't get back up.

Henry wanted to take a moment to enjoy knowing that he had stopped a madman, but just as he thought about it, he remembered that Calvin had been trying to inspire loyalty.

At the sound of feet hitting pavement toward the front of the house, he hoped that loyalty hadn't stuck.

He had no weapons.

His hands were cuffed behind his back.

His shirt was soaked from the blood pouring out of his multiple wounds.

But he had two women to save, another woman to find and a son he very much wanted to raise.

Henry spun around, ready to win every fight he had to, to see all those things come to pass.

"Henry!"

But it was Cassie who was running toward him, her sister and Maggie behind her. Michael was there, too. Gun out.

Cassie must have seen the look he was giving the man.

"He's a good guy," she told him, nearly closing the space between them.

Henry was about to question that when the red-haired man lifted his gun up and aimed it at them. Henry took a step forward, already imagining using his body as a shield to keep Cassie safe, when the world seemed to go into slow motion.

Green eyes, the color of a forest after a nice, cleansing rain, widened in fear. It wasn't at Henry. It was behind him.

Without turning around he realized he'd fallen for Calvin's deceit one last time.

The man who had pretended to die by gunshots in a barn in Tennessee had pretended once again that he had been beaten.

Henry turned, knowing that Calvin would wait until he saw Henry's defeat before he pulled the trigger. Then, when he was done with Henry, he'd just as surely shoot Cassie before Michael could do anything about it.

And Henry refused to let anyone else suffer because of his past.

Cassie was already yelling by the time Henry turned. That yell turned into a scream by the time Henry had run at Calvin. He was sitting up but armed, as Henry had already guessed.

A gunshot filled the air around them as Henry took the bullet in the shoulder.

He didn't let it slow him down.

With every ounce of anger, remorse and guilt left in him, Henry kicked the gun free of Calvin's hand and then kicked the man.

Henry heard the crack and knew it was the one that would end his old partner.

Calvin fell back onto the remnants of the broken window, neck at an odd angle, eyes open and unblinking, looking up toward the sky.

Henry hoped that his best friend had finally found peace.

Even if it was more than he deserved.

"Henry!"

The bulge of a pregnant belly brushed up against Henry's bound hands. Darkness might have tinted the edges of his vision, bullets and cuts and bruises might have been trying to work together to bring him down, but in that moment Henry finally felt his own version of peace.

# Epilogue

Cassie looked down and sighed. The white fabric clung to a stomach that wasn't flat but definitely didn't have a curve to it anymore. She fanned her fingers across the beads Kristen had been so insistent about. The dress was gorgeous, but still she found her form was lacking.

Kristen laughed from the doorway. "You know, I'm sure if you asked nicely, that husband of yours might just put another baby in there."

Cassie rolled her eyes but couldn't deny the idea was appealing.

"I think it might be nice to wait until *at least* a day after the wedding," she said. "Don't you think?"

Kristen waved off her concern. "I mean, technically, the wedding *is* over." She motioned to the window. Through the slats in the plantation shutter a party of people could be seen milling around outside. "The reception *has* already started."

Cassie felt her lips curve into a smile. It was genuine and one of many that had taken place during the course of the afternoon.

Six months had passed since Calvin Fitzgerald had died on the grass in between two houses in Westbridge. Six months since a terrified Cassie had held a bleeding Henry in her arms until an ambulance had gotten to them. Six months since she had thought she might lose the love of her life forever.

That day the communications of the department might have been lacking, but it hadn't mattered in the end. Whether following his instincts or his heart, Detective Matt Walker had decided to revisit Westbridge in pursuit of his fiancée. He'd showed up to find her, Kristen, Michael and the two lackeys they'd incapacitated in the street. He'd sent the cavalry in as soon as he'd spotted the group. Until they arrived, Henry had stayed conscious and, somehow, had found enough left in him to scold Cassie.

"I'd appreciate it if you'd stop trying to rescue me," he'd said, a smile on his lips.

Cassie had shushed him. "I'm a Southern lady. We're only polite until someone threatens what's ours. You're mine, Deputy Ward. If you're in trouble, then know I'll always be right there trying to get you out of it."

He'd laughed. "I could get used to that."

She'd ridden to the hospital with him, Kristen in tow, and spent every day at his side as he'd recovered from his wounds. Then, two months later, their places had reversed. However, that was all thanks to a blond-haired, green-eyed baby boy named Colby.

If you asked Henry if he had cried the first time

he'd seen his son, he would shake his head, but Cassie knew differently.

He'd been putty in Colby's tiny hands since minute one.

Cassie caught sight of her sister, Denise, homing in on the very man who had stolen her heart. She let out a sigh. "I suppose I should get back out there and save that poor man from being cornered by Denise."

Kristen came up beside her and put an arm across her shoulders.

"You know, if you really wanted her to, I bet she'd move back here if you asked," she said. "She *is* the responsible sister. I bet she'd make life a lot easier, since she has a bunch of kids, too."

Cassie shook her head and nudged the woman next to her. "I love her, just like I know you do, too, but I think the only sibling I need already lives across the street."

Kristen's cheeks dimpled as a huge smile stretched over her face. She squeezed her shoulders and then, just as quickly, she turned to teasing. "All right, Mrs. Ward. Stop being all emotional and let's go save your husband from the wonderful terror that is our Denise."

The dance floor was filled to the brim with people, just as the many tables were. Cassie had opted for a smaller wedding, but Henry had refused. He'd known how much her family meant to her and since they were their own large crowd, half the place belonged to them. The other half had been split between Henry's small family and the Riker County Sheriff's Department. Almost everyone had found a way to come or to stop by. Others had to ask for time off, considering they were in the wedding.

Cassie smiled from her spot at a table near the dance floor where she'd needed to rest. From there she got an uninhibited view of Billy dancing with his daughter while Mara danced with their son. Matt, Maggie and their son were getting down next to them while Suzy, James and their large family did their own version of getting down.

Cassie spotted Kristen near the outside, wondering if the woman was pining after the good-looking millionaire, but surprised to see all her attention on a different man.

"Oh, boy," she muttered to herself. Kristen was using her flirty smile on none other than Garrett, Henry's brother. *That* was going to be interesting. Especially since Garrett had just surprised Henry with the news that he was transferring to Darby.

"Listen, I need you to buy me a drink."

Cassie's smile doubled as the sound of her husband's voice brushed against her ear.

"I need you to pretend to buy me a drink, that is," he said, quoting what she'd said to Gary at the Eagle. It seemed like a lifetime ago.

"I don't know if my husband would like that," she said, watching him step around her and take the seat at her side. In his arms was the only other man who could ever look so good in a suit.

"I don't think he would mind. Especially since he probably deserves one after dealing with the particularly dangerous diaper he just changed." He gave her a smirk, the one that made every part of her stand at attention. If he'd been wearing his blue jeans, Cassie might just have melted completely.

Henry passed Colby over and then readjusted his chair so they both could look out over the dance floor.

Cassie ran her hand through her baby boy's soft hair while Henry stroked the back of her shoulder with his thumb.

"I could get used to this," she finally said, feeling the full force of contented happiness in being surrounded by her love, her heart and her family.

Henry smiled.

"Good," he said. "Because I don't intend to ever let you go. I might be an idiot sometimes, but I'm not *that* stupid."

And then that smirk came right on back.

Maybe she didn't need him to be wearing those blue jeans after all.

\* \* \* \* \*

*Look for the next book in Tyler Anne Snell's*
*The Protectors of Riker County*
*miniseries,* The Negotiation,
*available next month.*

*And don't miss the previous titles in*
*The Protectors of Riker County series:*

Small-Town Face-Off
The Deputy's Witness
Forgotten Pieces
Loving Baby

*Available now from Harlequin Intrigue!*

## COMING NEXT MONTH FROM

### ⬢ HARLEQUIN®

# INTRIGUE

### Available August 21, 2018

### #1803 HARD RUSTLER
*Whitehorse, Montana: The Clementine Sisters* • by B.J. Daniels
For Dawson Rogers, Annabelle "Annie" Clementine is the one who got away. Now she's returned to sell her grandmother's house. Dawson can't help coming to her rescue, especially when he realizes that the house isn't the only thing her grandmother left her—Annie also inherited a mystery.

### #1804 FINGER ON THE TRIGGER
*The Lawmen of McCall Canyon* • by Delores Fossen
When rancher Rachel McCall has a one-night stand with longtime friend Texas Ranger Griff Morris, it starts a deadly chain of events that puts them in the crosshairs of a killer.

### #1805 FOUR RELENTLESS DAYS
*Mission: Six* • by Elle James
Navy SEAL "Harm" Harmon Payne and beautiful safari resort owner Talia Ryan are caught in a web of danger when poachers threaten the resort, the animals and the lives of those trying to protect them.

### #1806 IN THE LAWMAN'S PROTECTION
*Omega Sector: Under Siege* • by Janie Crouch
A terrorist is on the loose, and agent Ren McClement will do anything to stop him, including using the terrorist's ex-wife, Natalie Anderson, as bait. Before long, he realizes Natalie's innocent, and now he'll do whatever it takes to keep her safe—especially since he's the one who put her in danger.

### #1807 DEPUTY DEFENDER
*Eagle Mountain Murder Mystery* • by Cindi Myers
When someone threatens Brenda Stenson's life and livelihood, she turns to her childhood friend Deputy Dwight Prentice for help. Can Dwight stop her stalker before it's too late?

### #1808 THE NEGOTIATION
*The Protectors of Riker County* • by Tyler Anne Snell
After someone attempts to abduct Rachel Roberts, she seeks help from Dane Jones, the captain at the sheriff's department and Rachel's deceased husband's best friend. Dane and Rachel must work together to overcome their shared past and decide if they can finally be together in the future.

**YOU CAN FIND MORE INFORMATION ON UPCOMING HARLEQUIN® TITLES, FREE EXCERPTS AND MORE AT WWW.HARLEQUIN.COM.**

HICNM0818

As her sports car topped the rise, Annabelle Clementine looked
out at the rugged country spread before her and felt her heart
drop. She'd never thought she'd see so many miles of wild
winter Montana landscape ever again. At least, she'd hoped not.

How could she have forgotten the remoteness? The vastness?
The isolation? There wasn't a town in sight. Or a ranch house. Or
another living soul.

She glanced down at her gas gauge. It hovered at empty. She'd
tried to get gas at the last station, but her credit card wouldn't
work and she'd gone through almost all of her cash. She'd put in
what fuel she could with the change she was able to scrape up,
but it had barely moved the gauge. If she ran out of gas before she
reached Whitehorse…well, it would just be her luck, wouldn't it?

She let the expensive silver sports car coast down the mountain
toward the deep gorge of the Missouri River, thankful that most
of the snow was high in the mountains and not on the highway.
She didn't know what she would have done if the roads had been
icy since she hadn't seen a snow tire since she'd left Montana.

The motor coughed. She looked down at the gauge. The
engine had to be running on fumes. What was she going to do?
It was still miles to Whitehorse. Tears burned her eyes, but she

refused to cry. Yes, things were bad. Really bad. But—

She was almost to the river bottom when she saw it. At a wide spot where the river wound on its way through Montana east to the Mississippi, a pickup and horse trailer were pulled off to the side of the highway. Her pulse jumped at just the thought of another human being—let alone the possibility of getting some fuel. If she could just get to Whitehorse…

But as she descended the mountain, she didn't see anyone around the pickup or horse trailer. What if the rig had been left beside the road and the driver was nowhere to be found? Maybe there would be a gas can in the back of the pickup or— *Have you stooped so low that now you would steal gas?*

Fortunately, she wasn't forced to answer that. She spotted a cowboy standing on the far side of the truck. Her instant of relief was quickly doused as she looked around and realized how alone the two of them were, out here in the middle of nowhere.

*Don't be silly. What are the chances the cowboy is a serial killer, rapist, kidnapper, ax murderer…?* The motor sputtered as if taking its last gasp as she slowed. It wasn't as if she had a choice. She hadn't seen another car for over an hour. For miles she'd driven through open country dotted occasionally with cows but no people. And she knew there was nothing but rugged country the rest of the way north to Whitehorse.

If there had been any other way to get where she was headed, she would have taken it. But her options had been limited for some time now.

And today, it seemed, her options had come down to this cowboy and possible serial killer rapist kidnapper ax murderer.

*Don't miss* Hard Rustler *by B.J. Daniels,
available September 2018 wherever
Harlequin® Intrigue books and ebooks are sold.*

www.Harlequin.com

# SPECIAL EXCERPT FROM

*Hawk Cahill let down Deidre "Drey" Hunter
once before. He isn't going to make that mistake again,
especially since she just married the wrong man—a man
who is suddenly missing.*

*Read on for a sneak preview of
RANCHER'S DREAM,
the next book in* **THE MONTANA CAHILLS** *series
by* New York Times *bestselling author B.J. Daniels.*

*You will die in this house.*

The thought seemed to rush out of the darkness as the house came into view. The premonition turned her skin clammy. Drey gripped a handful of her wedding dress, her fingers aching but unable to release the expensive fabric as she stared at her new home. A wedding gift, Ethan had said. A surprise, sprung on her at the reception.

The portent still had a death grip on her. She could see herself lying facedown in a pool of water, her auburn hair fanned out around her head, her body so pale it appeared to have been drained of all blood.

"Are you all right?" her husband asked now as he reached over to take her hand. "Dierdre?" Unlike everyone else she knew, Ethan refused to call her by her nickname, Drey

"I'm still a little woozy from the reception," she said, desperately needing fresh air right now as she put down her window to let in the cool Montana summer night.

"I warned you about drinking too much champagne."

He'd warned her about a lot of things. But it wasn't the champagne, which she hadn't touched during the reception. He knew she didn't drink, but he'd insisted one glass of champagne at her wedding wasn't going to kill her. She'd gotten one of the waiters to bring her sparkling cider.

So it wasn't alcohol that had her stomach roiling. No, it was when Ethan told her where they would be living. She'd assumed they would live in his New York City penthouse since that was where he spent most of his time. She'd actually been looking forward to it because she'd grown up in Gilt Edge, Montana, and had never lived in a large city before. Also it would be miles from Gilt Edge—and Hawk Cahill.

She'd never dreamed that Ethan meant for them to live here in Montana, at the place he'd named Mountain Crest. All during construction, she'd thought that the odd structure was to be used as a business retreat only. Ethan had been so proud of the high-tech house with its barred gate at the end of the paved road, she'd never let on that she knew the locals made fun of it—and its builder.

When Ethan had pulled her aside at the reception and told her that they would be living on the mountain overlooking Gilt Edge in his prized house, Dierdre hadn't been able to hide her shock. She'd never dreamed… But then she'd never dreamed she would be married to Ethan Baxter.

*Don't miss RANCHER'S DREAM*
*by B.J. Daniels, available now wherever*
*Harlequin® books and ebooks are sold.*

www.Harlequin.com